The Mamur Zapt and the Spoils of Egypt

But what, Captain Owen asked himself, was Miss Skinner doing looking at crocodiles? Especially, mummified ones? It mattered because Miss Skinner was a lady with a habit of asking awkward questions. And because her uncle might, just might, become the next President of the United States, those questions had to be answered. At present they were concentrated on the illegal export of antiquities. And Owen, the Mamur Zapt, or Head of Cairo's Secret Police, had just been given the task of seeing that Egypt's priceless antiquities stayed in Egypt.

But were they priceless? Were they even antiquities? At times it seemed that the whole of Egypt was engaged in one dubious aspect or other of the antiquities business. And what about Miss Skinner herself? When she so narrowly escaped falling under a Cairo tram, was it because she had been nudged by a fat-tailed Passover sheep? Or by something more sinister?

These were minor problems compared to those which later faced Owen. As he fought to halt the flight abroad of Egypt's national treasures he had also to decide whether to ask Zeinab to marry him. And how to differentiate between archæology and plunder.

by the same author

THE MAMUR ZAPT AND THE GIRL IN THE NILE
THE MAMUR ZAPT AND THE MEN BEHIND
THE MAMUR ZAPT AND THE DONKEY-VOUS
THE MAMUR ZAPT AND THE NIGHT OF THE DOG
THE MAMUR ZAPT AND THE RETURN OF THE CARPET

MICHAEL PEARCE

The Mamur Zapt and the Spoils of Egypt

THE CRIME CLUB
An Imprint of HarperCollins *Publishers*

First published in Great Britain in 1992
by The Crime Club, an imprint of
HarperCollins Publishers, 77–85 Fulham Palace Road,
Hammersmith, London W6 8JB

9 8 7 6 5 4 3 2 1

Michael Pearce asserts the moral right to be identified
as the author of this work.

© Michael Pearce 1992

A catalogue record for this book is
available from the British Library

ISBN 0 00 232417 2

Photoset in Linotron Baskerville by
Rowland Phototypesetting Ltd
Bury St Edmunds, Suffolk
Printed and bound in Great Britain by
HarperCollins Book Manufacturing, Glasgow

CHAPTER 1

A tall, thin, angular woman came through the door of the hotel.

Immediately a hand was thrust up at her. It was holding something grey, crumbly and rubbery—rather like old fish —from which a faint aroma arose.

'What is this?' she said, sniffing suspiciously.

'Real mummy!' said the voice behind the hand. 'Genuine mummy flesh! Only ten piastres!'

'Thank you, no!' said the woman firmly.

Her initial hesitation, however, proved fatal. In a moment they were all round her. Other hands pushed out brandishing bits of bandage (mummy linen), bits of wood (mummy coffin), bright blue saucers straight from the tombs (well, near them, at any rate), genuine old scarab beetles (and some of them were), little wooden images of the gods, little clay images of scribes (such is our fate), little plaques of rough clay engraved with religious images and little coloured wooden Ships of the Dead.

She tried to brush past.

Something was held up in front of her to block her way. It was a mummified arm, complete with fingers.

As she recoiled, a voice said: 'For you, Madame, for you!'

'I don't think so.'

'For you especially!' the man insisted.

'Thank you, no.'

A young man in a white European suit and a fez came through the door behind her and at once released a torrent of Arabic so impressive that even the hardened owners of the hands were taken aback. The porters lounging at the doorway, shaken, rushed forward and chivvied them from the terrace.

'Why, thank you, Mr Trevelyan!' said the lady in a cool American voice. 'You come to my rescue yet again!'

The young man bowed.

'A pleasure, Miss Skinner.'

He looked up and saw the man sitting on the terrace.

'Gareth!' he said. 'This is a bit of luck!'

Owen had just been thinking how nice it was to see so many old swindlers of his acquaintance back in town, only that day arrived from Upper Egypt where they had been passing the winter selling pillaged or fabricated antiques to the tourists on Cook's Nile steamers. He recognized some of the old faithfuls. That surely was—

And then Paul Trevelyan had come through the door.

'Gareth! There's someone I'd like you to meet.'

He shepherded the woman across.

'Captain Owen,' he said, 'the Mamur Zapt.'

Owen rose.

'Miss Skinner.'

'Pleased to meet you, Captain Owen,' she said, extending a hand, then sitting down in one of the chairs opposite him. 'But who or what is the Mamur Zapt?'

'It's the traditional Arabic title of the post I hold.'

'And what post is that?'

'It's a kind of police post.'

'You are a policeman?'

'Yes,' said Owen, 'yes. You could say that.'

The woman frowned slightly. She was about thirty and had a long, thin, sharp face. Sharp eyes, too.

'There seems some doubt about it,' she said.

Paul Trevelyan came to his assistance.

'Captain Owen looks after the political side,' he explained.

'The post was originally Head of the Khedive's Secret Police,' said Owen.

'Ah!'

'But, of course, things are very different now.'

They certainly were. For this was 1908 and although the Khedive was still the nominal ruler of Egypt and Egypt was still nominally an autonomous province of the Ottoman Empire, the Ottomans were no longer in power.

Nor were the Egyptians, for that matter. The new rulers of Egypt were the British, who had come into the country thirty years before to help the Khedive sort out his chaotic finances: come and stayed.

'The British seem everywhere,' said Miss Skinner.

'Oh, I wouldn't say that. We're advisers only, you know.'

'Really?'

'Oh yes.'

'And you yourself,' said Miss Skinner pointedly, 'you are an adviser, too?'

'Yes.'

'Whom do you advise?'

'Oh, lots of people. The Khedive—'

Formally, that was.

'The Chief of Police—'

Who happened to be British.

'Mr Trevelyan's boss?' asked Miss Skinner.

The Consul-General. The British Consul-General, that was. The man who really ran Egypt.

'You could say that,' said Owen, smiling.

'I get the picture,' said Miss Skinner.

'Miss Skinner's interests are archæological,' said Paul firmly, deciding that it was time to re-route her.

'And statistical,' corrected Miss Skinner. 'There are a number of things I wish to look into while I am here.'

Behind her back Paul raised his eyes heavenwards.

'I am sure our Finance Department will be glad to help you,' said Owen, who had a grudge against the Finance Department.

Miss Skinner pursed her lips.

'It is the flesh and blood behind the statistics that

interests me. I am not sure that Finance Departments are so good at that.'

'I am taking Miss Skinner to see some of the excavations,' said Paul doggedly.

'Fascinating!' said Owen.

The vendors of antiquities, recovered, had regrouped in front of the terrace and were now beginning to slide their wares beseechingly through the railings. Miss Skinner looked down.

'Fake!' she pronounced.

'But nice, don't you think?' said Owen, who rather liked the blue scarab beetles and admired the workmanship that went into the barques.

'I am only,' said Miss Skinner, 'interested in the truth.'

There was something of a pause.

'And where,' asked Owen chattily, seeing signs of desperation in Paul, 'were you planning to go?'

'Der el Bahari, primarily.'

'Oh, there are lots of things to see there. You'll find it very interesting,' Owen assured Miss Skinner.

'There's an American team up there at the moment,' said Paul. 'I gather they're making some promising finds.'

'I know Parker,' said Miss Skinner. 'I'm afraid I don't like his methodology.'

'Ah well,' said Owen, 'you'll be able to help him put it right, then.'

He felt something touching his foot and glanced down. A particularly resourceful vendor had laid out some *ushapti* images on a piece of coffin and was poking it under the table for them to see.

Miss Skinner picked up one of the images and turned it over between her hands. She seemed puzzled.

'It looks genuine,' she said, 'but—'

'It probably *is* genuine.'

'But how can that be?'

Owen shrugged.

'It might even come from Der el Bahari. That's where a lot of these men came from.'

Miss Skinner's eyes widened.

'You mean—these things are *stolen*.'

'Accumulated, say. Perhaps even over the centuries. The ancestors of these men, Miss Skinner, built the temples and tombs in the Valley of Kings. And ever since they have been, well, revenging themselves on their masters.'

'Then they are grave-robbers,' cried Miss Skinner, 'and must be stopped!'

As Paul piloted Miss Skinner down the steps, the vendors closed in again. The man with the mummified arm pushed his way through the crowd and waved it once more in her face.

'For you, Madame, for you!'

'No,' said Miss Skinner, 'no.'

'For you especially,' the man insisted.

'Grave-robbers!' said Monsieur Peripoulin hotly. 'That's what they are!'

'Oh, come—'

'That's what they are!' the Frenchman insisted. The sweat was running down his face, which wasn't surprising since he was wearing a dark suit and a stiff, high, white collar, which was, apparently, what he always wore at the Museum.

'Just tourists,' said Owen.

'Not the ones I'm talking about,' Monsieur Peripoulin declared. 'Tourists go to the bazaars and buy a few souvenirs. These men usually go straight to the excavations and buy there.'

'They can't, surely,' said Paul. 'Excavations are closely controlled these days and all finds have to be listed and reported to the Director of Antiquities.'

'Closely controlled!' said Monsieur Peripoulin scathingly. 'If you believe that, you'll believe anything!'

Paul sighed. The meeting had been going on for two and a half hours now and it was past midday. He had been relying on the French habit of dropping everything at noon and going for lunch, but the elderly Frenchman seemed as determined as ever.

'What exactly, Monsieur Peripoulin, are you proposing?' he asked wearily.

'A licence system,' said the Frenchman immediately. 'That is what we need. Anyone wishing to export an antiquity should have to obtain a licence first.'

'Don't we have that already?' asked Carmichael, from Customs. 'Or the next best thing to it. If anyone wishes to export antiquities they have to send them first to the Museum.'

'Yes, but that's only to determine export duty,' said Monsieur Peripoulin. 'We put a value on it—and that's not always easy, let me tell you: what value would you put on the Sphinx?—seal the case and notify the Mudir of Customs.'

'What's wrong with that?' asked the man from Customs.

'It just goes ahead automatically. No one makes a conscious decision.'

'We make a decision,' said Carmichael. 'We decide what level of duty applies.'

'Yes, but you don't ask yourselves whether in principle the thing should be exported at all. It's that kind of decision I'm talking about.'

'Just a minute,' said Paul, chairing the meeting on behalf of the Consul-General. 'Are you suggesting that we should interfere with the free flow of trade?'

'These things cannot be seen solely in terms of money,' declared Monsieur Peripoulin stoutly. 'They are part of Egypt's priceless heritage.'

'I quite agree,' said the man from Finance: an Egyptian. He was an Under-Secretary—which was a sign that someone somewhere was taking the meeting seriously—and his name was Abu Bakir.

Paul raised an eyebrow.

'Naturally, works of art have an intrinsic value,' he said smoothly. 'Once they are on the market, however, they have a market value.'

'The question is: how do they get on the market?' said Abu Bakir.

'It is not their value that I am concerned about,' said Monsieur Peripoulin, 'but their location.'

'That, too, is determined by the market.'

'But ought it to be? That is what I am asking. It is an issue of principle,' the Frenchman insisted.

'Yes,' said Paul, 'but which principle? At this stage in Egypt's development I would have thought the overriding necessity was to ensure Egypt's economic health. And that is best done by adherence to the principles of Free Trade.'

'I am afraid,' said the Egyptian, who was, after all, from the Ministry of Finance, 'that I have to agree.'

'What?' cried Monsieur Peripoulin, throwing up his hands in dismay. 'You are willing to see Egypt's treasures disappear?'

'I did not say that,' said Abu Bakir. 'I did not say that.' He turned to Paul. 'Can we return for a moment to a distinction Monsieur Peripoulin made earlier?'

'What distinction?' said Paul, glancing at his watch.

'The one between the ordinary tourist and the specialist buyer. As far as the ordinary tourist is concerned, I think I agree with you: we should not interfere in the ordinary processes of trade. With respect to the specialist buyer and the exceptional item, however, I find myself tempted by Monsieur Peripoulin's licensing proposal.'

'I don't think we can take a decision on something as major as that today.'

'Perhaps not, but I don't think we ought just to leave it. Perhaps we can ask Customs to look into it and report back?'

'We could do that,' assented Paul.

It being past lunch-time, everyone was prepared to agree and the meeting broke up. As they walked out, Monsieur Peripoulin put a hot hand on Owen's arm.

'All this is missing the point. Licence, not licence, that is not the point. What happens when the goods don't come to us at all?'

'They should all come to you.'

'But what happens when they don't?'

'Ah well,' said Abu Bakir over Owen's shoulder, 'that's where the Mamur Zapt comes in.'

'Not the Mamur Zapt; the police,' said Owen.

'The police!' said Monsieur Peripoulin dismissively.

'I'm inclined to agree with you,' said Carmichael, from Customs. 'The police can't do much about it. Half the staff goes out under Capitulatory privilege.'

'That's why I said the Mamur Zapt,' said Abu Bakir.

'I don't want to have anything to do with it,' said Owen.

'Very sensible of you,' said Paul.

'If it's tied up with the Capitulations we won't get anywhere.'

The Capitulations were privileges granted to European powers by successive Ottoman rulers in return for organizing international trade.

'True,' said Paul.

'In that case that's something for the Foreign Office, not me.'

'Mm,' said Paul.

'In fact, I wonder why I was there at all. Who called the meeting?'

'I did.'

'You did?' said Owen, surprised.

They were at a reception that evening in what Old India hands called the Residency and new English ones the Consulate-General. The house was, indeed, in the style of English building in India, designed to protect against the heat rather than against the cold. The floor was tiled, the roof domed, the windows shuttered and the doors arched. Through one of the arches Owen could see Miss Skinner talking to Abu Bakir.

'Yes. It's moving up the political agenda.'

'The export of antiquities?'

'People are getting interested.'

'What people? Peripoulin goes on about it, I know, but—'

'Other people. People outside Egypt.'

'They're the ones who are buying the stuff!'

'Yes. But other ones are asking questions about it.'

'About us exporting antiquities?'

'And other things, too. About our stewardship, for instance, of Egyptian treasures.'

'We're looking after them all right, aren't we? Old Peripoulin—'

'We're selling them off. At least, that's how some people see it.'

'*We're* not selling them off. Private individuals are. That's nothing to do with us.'

'Isn't it? Some people think it is. Some people think there ought to be a regulatory framework.'

'I see. So that's what the meeting was about.'

'It's very important,' said Paul, 'that people get the right impression.'

'Maybe. I still don't see why I had to be there, though.'

Paul smiled.

Across the room Miss Skinner was now talking to Peripoulin and another Frenchman, L'Espinasse, the Inspector of Antiquities.

'There's that damned woman. Why are you spending time on her, Paul?'

'Her uncle could be the next President of the United States.'

'Really?'

'If he wins the election in a year's time. He's sent her out here on a fact-finding mission.'

'You'd better make sure she finds the right facts, then.'

'I am sticking to her like glue,' said Paul.

Miss Skinner came towards them.

'Perhaps you gentlemen can explain to me why it is that all the people in the Antiquities Service are French? No, don't tell me! Can it be that the English concentrate on the money and leave the culture to the French?'

'Shame, Miss Skinner! There are eminent English archæologists working in the service, too!'

'And are there Frenchmen working in the Ministry of Finance?'

'We work a lot in French,' said Paul truthfully but evading the point. 'Egypt's links with France go back to the time of Napoleon.'

'The first of the spoilers!' declared Miss Skinner. She waved a hand at Owen as she moved away. 'I'm so looking forward to tomorrow!'

'What's this?' said Owen.

Paul looked uncomfortable.

'I was hoping you'd come round for a drink.'

'Certainly.'

'And bring Zeinab.'

'Certainly. But why particularly bring Zeinab?'

'Miss Skinner would like to meet her.'

'She's never heard of Zeinab. Unless you've been telling her!'

'She wants to meet an Egyptian woman. An *ordinary* Egyptian woman.'

'Well, Zeinab's not exactly ordinary—'

'She's the nearest I can get. You won't believe how difficult it is in Egypt to meet an ordinary woman.'

'I'll see if she's free,' promised Owen.

'I'm trying to get Miss Skinner's mind off antiquities. The Woman Question is my big hope.'

'Just a minute: antiquities. One of Miss Skinner's hobby-horses doesn't happen to be the export of Egypt's treasures, does it?'

'As a matter of fact,' said Paul, 'I believe it does.'

Monsieur Peripoulin bestowed a fatherly pat as he went past.

'A useful meeting!' he said. 'At last things are beginning to move.'

'That meeting,' said Owen, 'it wouldn't have anything to do with Miss Skinner's being here, would it? The fact that you called it, I mean?'

'It's been in our minds a long time,' said Paul.

Some time later in the evening Owen came upon Miss Skinner and Abu Bakir having an earnest chat in one of the alcoves.

'I was just explaining to Mr Bakir,' said Miss Skinner, her face slightly flushed, 'that my friends and I are very concerned about the fact that so many of Egypt's remarkable treasures are departing her shores.'

'And I was explaining to Miss Skinner,' said Abu Bakir, smiling, 'that many of us in Egypt are concerned about that also.'

'True,' said Owen, 'very true.'

'Mr Bakir was explaining to me the Nationalist position.'

'Not just the Nationalist position,' said Abu Bakir quickly, his smile disappearing. 'It is one, I believe, that the Nationalists share with the Government.'

'Although, as you were saying, the vested interests of the big landlords make it very difficult to get anything through the Assembly.'

'I was giving Miss Skinner some of the political background,' Abu Bakir explained.

I'll bet you were, thought Owen.

'There are political difficulties, it is true,' he said out loud, 'but I think we're beginning to face them.'

'Yes,' said Miss Skinner, 'Monsieur Peripoulin was tell-ing me about some meeting you had had recently.'

'Oh yes,' said Owen. 'a very important meeting.'

'Meetings are all very well,' said Miss Skinner, frowning, 'but it's the action that results from them that is important. I understand, for instance, that there is a widespread eva-sion of the controls on the export of antiquities. What is being done about that?'

'Ah,' said Abu Bakir, 'but that is just where we are taking action. The Mamur Zapt—Captain Owen here—is about to take steps to stamp that out.'

'Are you?' said Miss Skinner, beaming. 'Oh, I'm so glad. I shall follow what you do with great interest.'

Owen was sitting in a café in the Ataba-el-Khadra watching the world go by. The Ataba was a good place for that because it was at the end of the main street, the Muski, which connected the old native city with the new European quarters. The square was, moreover, the main terminus for nearly all of Cairo's trams.

At any hour of the day and deep into the night the Ataba was a tangle of trams, arabeahs—the characteristic horse-drawn cab of Cairo—great lumbering carts carrying stone, great lumbering camels carrying forage for the city's don-keys and horses, native buses, of the open-sided ass-drawn variety, motor-cars (a few; tending towards the stationary) and sheep.

Quite why there should be so many sheep in the Ataba was a mystery. Certainly the Arabs were very fond of their fat-tailed Passover sheep and shopkeepers liked to keep one tethered outside their premises, to eat up the garbage, it was claimed; but why so many should be wandering loose in this most hazardous of places was hard to comprehend.

You would feel something nudging your knee and look down and there would be a sheep painted in blue stripes and often with a child's shoe hanging round its neck on a cheap silver necklace.

The answer lay, perhaps, in the fact that despite the trams and despite its proximity to the new European quarters the Ataba remained obstinately part of the native city. The people you saw were the ordinary people of Cairo: blue-gowned labourers, veiled women in black, office workers in suits and tarbooshes, the red, pot-like hat of the educated Egyptian, shopkeepers in striped gowns and tarbooshes but with a turban bound round the tarboosh.

The hawkers, too, of whom there were very many, were ones who served the ordinary Egyptian rather than the tourist. Instead of the souvenir-seller and dirty-postcard-seller of the great hotels you saw the brush, comb and buttonhook-seller, the pastry-seller, the lemonade-seller and the water-carrier.

It was two different worlds and despite the incessant clanging of the trams and the shouts of the street vendors Owen on the whole preferred this one to the hotel one.

He had been visiting the fire station on the Ataba and afterwards had adjourned with the chief, as was proper after transacting business, to the coffee house. They sat there now benignly watching the mêlée in the square.

'So what would you do,' asked Owen, 'if you wanted to get out and your way was blocked?'

'I would ring my bell and shout.'

'But nearly everyone else in the square is ringing a bell and shouting,' Owen pointed out.

'I would exhort them,' said the Fire Chief.

And by the time you got anywhere, thought Owen, half the city would have burned to the ground.

'Is there no other exit?'

The Fire Chief pushed back his tarboosh and scratched his head.

'Well—' he was just beginning, when on the other side of the square there was a fierce squeal of brakes and a tram-bell started jangling furiously. An arabeah veered suddenly and there were agitated shouts.

A crowd seemed to be gathering in front of one of the trams. It looked as if there had been an accident.

A policeman somewhere was blowing his whistle. Owen could see him now pushing his way through the crowd. The crowd, unusually, parted and Owen caught a glimpse of a still form lying beside the tram.

It seemed to be a woman, a European.

He got to his feet. The Fire Chief, used to dealing with accidents, fell in beside him. Together they began to force a way through the crowd.

Even in that short time it had grown enormously. It was now well over a hundred deep. Traffic everywhere had come to a stop.

Some of the other trams had started ringing their bells. People were shouting, sheep bleating. As ass began to bray. It was bedlam.

The whole square now was an impenetrable mass of people. Owen looked at the Fire Chief and shrugged.

Over to one side was a native bus, totally becalmed. The driver had given up, laid his whip across the backs of his asses and was waiting resignedly. His passengers, content to watch the spectacle—all Cairo loved a good accident— chattered with excitement.

The Chief laid his hand on Owen's arm and nodded in the direction of the bus. They made their way towards it.

The bus was one of the traditional sort and was basically a platform on wheels. From the corners of the platform tall posts rose to support a roof. The sides were open and the wooden benches faced towards the rear.

The Chief put his foot on the running-board and jumped up. The next moment he was shinning nimbly up one of the posts and clambering on to the roof.

Owen followed, less nimbly. For an instant one foot hovered desperately in the air. Then someone caught hold of it and gave a heave, the Chief caught his arm, and he levered himself up on to the roof.

He could see now right across the crowd. There was a little space beside the tram where some arabeah drivers and the conductor of the tram were holding back the crowd. The driver had collapsed against the side and was clasping his head in his hands, his face turned away.

The crowd by the tram suddenly eddied—a horse, it looked like, had objected to being hemmed in—and Owen caught another glimpse of the woman.

Something about her seemed familiar.

And the next moment he had slid to the ground and was fighting his way through the crowd towards her.

'Make way! Make way!'

Someone looked up at him and took it into their head that he was the doctor.

'Make way for the hakim!' he shouted. 'Make way!'

Others took up the shout.

'The hakim! Make way!'

The crowd obligingly parted and hands tugged him through. He arrived dishevelled beside the tram and looked down. There, lying so close to the tram that she was almost beneath its running-boards, was Miss Skinner.

'I did not see her!' said the driver tearfully. 'I did not see her!'

Somebody had stuffed a jacket under her head and a water-carrier was tenderly, uselessly, splashing water on her face.

There was no blood.

'Get an ambulance!' said Owen.

The cry was taken up and passed through the crowd and at its back someone ran off into the café. But the Ataba was totally jammed and the ambulance, like the fire-engine, would be unable to get through.

And then, over the heads of the crowd, something was being passed, and there, scrambling over people's heads and shoulders, nimble as a monkey, was the Fire Chief.

A stretcher was passed down and, a moment later, the Chief arrived.

He dropped down on his knees beside Miss Skinner.

'God be praised!' he said.

'Be praised?' said Owen harshly.

'She is not dead.'

The Chief seized a water-skin from the carrier and squeezed some of the water out on to Miss Skinner's face.

Her eyes opened. For a moment they remained un-focused. And then the sharp look returned.

'What is going on?' demanded Miss Skinner.

'An accident,' said Owen. 'You've had an accident. Just stay there for a moment. You'll be all right.'

Miss Skinner's eyes closed again. The Fire Chief dexter-ously wedged the stretcher under her. Cooperative hands hoisted it into the air. It was raised head high so that it could be passed back over the crowd.

As the stretcher lurched upwards Miss Skinner's eyes opened again.

'Accident?' she said sharply. 'That was no accident! I was pushed!'

CHAPTER 2

'Look,' said Miss Skinner, 'I know a push when I feel one.'

She was sitting in a chair in the hotel lounge. Owen had suggested she remain in bed but Miss Skinner thought that was no place for a lady to receive a gentleman. She had made an appointment with Owen for six o'clock, taken a slightly extended siesta, and now here she was, not quite recovered—there was a nasty bruise on her face—but inclined in no sense to take this lying down.

'In the crowd,' murmured Owen, 'so easy to mistake—'

THE MAMUR ZAPT AND THE SPOILS OF EGYPT 21

Miss Skinner made an impatient gesture.

'A push is a push,' she said firmly.

'So many people,' said Owen, 'perhaps carrying things. A porter, maybe. A package sticking out.'

'A hand,' said Miss Skinner, 'gave me a deliberate push.'

Owen was silent. An image of the Ataba came into his mind. So many people milling about, jostling each other in the crowd, hurrying to catch a tram. The easiest thing in the world to bump into someone, collide. But a deliberate push?

'Let me see, Miss Skinner: you were standing precisely where? Near where I saw you, obviously, but, just before you fell, precisely where?'

'I had been looking at one of the boards—'

'Ah, so you had your back towards the traffic, then?'

'—but it was not the one I wanted and I had just turned away. I was looking for the one to the Zoological Gardens and this one, I remember, was for the Citadel. There! That will help you to place it.'

'Thank you. That is very precise. You had turned away, then—?'

'—and was about to move on to the next one when it happened.'

'That, again, is very precise, Miss Skinner. "About to move on." You had not, then, moved?'

'A step, perhaps.'

'Or two. But still very close to the Citadel board. And in the middle of the street.'

'Along with everybody else,' said Miss Skinner defensively.

'Of course. No criticism implied. But you were in the middle of the street and could very easily have been bumped into.'

'I think I would have noticed if an arabeah had hit me,' said Miss Skinner tartly. 'That is, of course, before I was hit by the tram.'

'I was thinking of a person, Miss Skinner. Perhaps running for a tram.'

Miss Skinner sighed.

'A collision is not like a push. This was a push. A definite push.'

'Perhaps as they collided with you they put out a hand—'

'No one,' said Miss Skinner, her voice beginning to rise, 'collided with me or bumped into me. What happened was that someone put a hand out and gave me a deliberate push just as the tram was approaching.'

'But, Miss Skinner, why would anyone want to do that?'

'You tell me. You're the policeman. If, indeed,' said Miss Skinner, 'you are a policeman!'

Owen could not see it. An accidental collision, a stumble, a trip, yes. But not a push. Not a deliberate push.

'A sheep, perhaps?' he ventured.

'A *sheep*?' said Miss Skinner incredulously.

'They nudge you,' Owen explained.

'Look, Captain Owen,' said Miss Skinner in rising fury, 'this was not a nudge, nor a bump, nor a jostle. This was a *push*. A hand. In the small of my back. Just when a tram was coming. I have been assaulted—criminally assaulted —and I demand that you take action to find out who my assailant was and to see that he is punished. At once!'

The arabeah-drivers, while waiting for custom, liked to gather round a pavement restaurant near where they parked their cabs; round, because what the restaurants consisted of was a large circular tray with little pegs round the edge on which the customers stuck their bread. In the middle were lots of little blue-and-white china bowls filled with various kinds of sauces and pickles and a few large platters on which lay unpromising pieces of meat.

The customers squatted round in the dust. They did not consist entirely of arabeah-drivers. The restaurant served as a social centre for that part of the Ataba and people dropped in and out all day, drawn by the smell of fried onions and the constant Arab need for sociability.

It was natural for Owen, beginning his inquiries with the arabeah-drivers, to migrate in that direction and soon he was part of the squatting circle dipping his bread with the rest of them, his inquiries now part of the general conversation.

'Why was she catching a tram anyway?' asked one of the arabeah-drivers. 'She ought to have been using an arabeah.'

'That's right. She wouldn't have had to have wandered round, then. She could have just signalled to us and we'd have looked after her.'

'Particularly if she was carrying things. Much more sense to take an arabeah.'

'*Was* she carrying things?' asked Owen.

'I don't know. It's just that if she was—'

'I thought she was carrying something,' said one of the other drivers. 'One or two small things. Perhaps she had been shopping.'

'You saw her, then?'

'I saw her go down. She certainly seemed to be carrying something.'

'How did she come to go down?' asked Owen. 'Was she wandering about in front of the tram or something?'

'No, no, she was round the side.'

'What did she do, then? Walk into it?' asked one of the drivers.

'Must have.'

'She ought to look where she's going, then.'

There was a general laugh.

'Maybe it came up behind her,' suggested Owen. 'You know, alongside her. She was standing a bit too close and it just caught her.'

'It's easily done, I suppose.'

Owen turned to the driver who had thought he'd seen her carrying something.

'Didn't you say you'd seen what happened? Was that how it was?'

'No, no, I didn't really see it happen. I just saw her go down. I had just cut across in front of the tram—plenty of room, a couple of metres at least—and of course I was looking out to my left and I glanced along the side of the tram and she was already falling. It must have happened just at that instant.'

'Was she falling into the tram or away from it?'

'I don't know, it was all over in a flash. But I saw she'd gone down as I stopped and ran over to her.'

'Was she all covered with blood?' asked someone with relish.

'No, she—'

The driver launched into his tale, which he told with gusto but without the kind of detail that interested Owen. After a while he stood up and slipped away. He would come back to the restaurant the next day and the days after. If anything new emerged it would certainly be retailed to him.

He went next to see the tram-driver, whom he found drinking tea with his fellows.

'It wasn't his fault!' they chorused. 'He couldn't have done anything about it. She just stepped straight into him.'

'You didn't see her coming?'

'How could I? She was down at the side.'

'You were moving, though. She must have been ahead of you.'

'Yes, but—'

'There were lots of people ahead of him! You can't see them all!'

'*Were* there lots of people? Was there a crowd?'

'There's always a crowd in the Ataba.'

'Yes, but was this woman part of a crowd or was she standing on her own?'

'I didn't see. I didn't see her at all until there was this

bump. You know at once. I jammed on my brakes and looked down and there she was!'

'It was the first time you'd seen her?'

'Of course! I swear on the Book—'

But then he would.

The conductor was strong in support.

'There were a lot of people milling about. There always are. And those stupid arabeah-drivers!'

'Yes, those stupid arabeah-drivers!'

'It's a wonder it doesn't happen more often.'

So not much joy there. Owen did a round of the stalls nearby, the tea stall, the sweet stall, the Arab sugar and Arab cucumber stalls, but although they all remembered the incident well—it had clearly made their day—and although all claimed to have been intimately involved, none of the owners, it transpired after some time, had actually seen anything.

Next he tried the street-sellers, many of whom had regular pitches and who, being more mobile than the stall-holders, had secured places near the front of the crowd. All of them, however, were observers after the event; somewhat to their regret.

They had at least seen something, though, and he tried to turn it to advantage. Could they describe the bystanders who had been at the front of the crowd, the ones who, presumably, had been nearest when the accident, or whatever it was, had happened?

Yes, they could: unfortunately, in implausible detail.

But did they *recognize* anybody?

'Don't I remember seeing Hamidullah?' the lemonade-seller asked himself.

'Hamidullah?'

'The carrier of water.'

'I remember a water-carrier,' said Owen.

'It would be him.'

'Where is he now?'

'Oh . . .'

The water-carrier, apparently, made long patrols of the town, passing through the Ataba three times a day, in the morning, afternoon and evening. Owen tried to establish the times more precisely.

The lemonade-seller did not possess a watch; could not, indeed, tell the time. Owen tried to get him to work it out in relation to the muezzin's call but then realized that one of the times, at any rate, he knew exactly. That was the one which coincided with Miss Skinner's fall. He would have to leave that now, however, till the next day.

Feeling that at least he had established something, and fed up at having had to spend most of the day on this daft business, he decided he'd had enough and went in to drink coffee with the Fire Chief.

'God be praised!' said the Fire Chief. 'You have come at last!'

Owen explained what he had been doing all day. The Chief, who must have seen him, affected surprise.

'Of course,' he said, 'I suppose you've got to look into it if it's a European.'

'Not all Europeans,' said Owen grimly. 'Just this one.'

'Are you going to punish the tram-driver?'

'Well, no, it wasn't really his fault.'

'All the same . . .' said the Fire Chief, casually conveying the centuries-old Cairene assumption that punishment was related more to the satisfaction of authority than to the desserts of offenders.

'From what I can make out,' said Owen, 'it doesn't seem to have been anybody's fault. It was just an accident.'

'What else?' said the Fire Chief.

What else, indeed? Even if it had been a push, it was almost certainly an unintended one. Miss Skinner had perhaps backed into somebody and they had merely warded her off. And then perhaps they had panicked when she had fallen over and made themselves scarce. He wished he could find someone who had seen what happened. If that was all, then they could forget about it.

It must have been something like that, an accidental jostle in the crowd, someone turning suddenly. What else could it be?

A deliberate push? That was ridiculous. Who would want to do a thing like that? Miss Skinner was unknown in Cairo. All right, in her short time here she had not exactly endeared herself to people, but hardly to the lengths of provoking someone to push her under a tram!

She was a European and Europeans were not exactly popular? Well, yes, but physical attacks on Europeans were few and far between. People fancied they occurred much more often than they actually did.

And that was probably it. Miss Skinner had almost certainly imagined the whole business. She didn't seem the fanciful sort, but you never could tell.

What else could it have been?

'I've got something for you,' said the Fire Chief.

He fished in a cupboard and produced a parasol and two or three small packages.

'Someone brought them to me,' he said. 'He found them under the tram, just where she had been lying.'

One of the packages was torn and Owen could see what was inside. It was a *ushapti* image of Osiris, about a foot tall and made in glazed faïence. It was well made but Owen was surprised. He pulled it out and turned it over in his hands.

'She'd been out shopping,' said the Fire Chief.

'Yes,' said Owen.

But why had she bought this? For this one, well made though it was, was still a fake.

The meeting with Zeinab had gone well; so well, that Miss Skinner expressed the wish to repeat it. And if possible in Zeinab's own home.

This proved a problem, for Zeinab had taken it for granted that the meeting would be in some such place as the terrace at Shepheard's, which was where one normally met. She had no intention of allowing anyone into her *appartement* other than Owen.

'What's the idea?' she said to Owen.

'I think she wants to see you in your natural habitat.'

'Shepheard's is my natural habitat,' said Zeinab.

'Yes, but she thinks you have a home.'

Zeinab considered.

'Perhaps we could meet at my father's,' she suggested.

Zeinab's father was a Pasha and possessed a town house, a fine old Mameluke building.

'I think—I think she had in mind an ordinary house.'

'This *is* an ordinary house,' said Zeinab, in a tone that brooked no argument.

'It will do fine,' said Paul hastily.

When, however, Owen arrived, shortly before the appointed hour, Zeinab was not there.

'I don't know where she is,' said Nuri Pasha, who had long ago given up attempting to keep track on his daughter's movements. He admired her deeply—she reminded him of her mother, his favourite courtesan—but understood her not at all.

'Miss Skinner will be arriving at any moment,' said Owen, consulting his watch.

'*Cette américaine,*' said Nuri a trifle anxiously, fearing that he was going to have to provide the entertainment on his own, '*est-elle jolie?*'

Owen had not really considered the matter. He did so now. Miss Skinner's trim form rose up before him; but also her sharp face.

'*Une jolie laide,*' he said at last, not wishing to discourage Nuri but feeling obliged to be truthful. Ugly-pretty.

'*Ah! C'est piquant, ça!*' said Nuri, intrigued. Like all upper-class Egyptians, he habitually spoke French.

'*Elle est formidable,*' Owen warned him.

Nuri brushed the warning aside. So long as the other parts of the equation were all right, the more *formidable* the better, so far as he was concerned. He liked a challenge.

Owen felt a little worried. Nuri's interests centred fairly narrowly on politics and sex and he was inclined to associate women exclusively with the latter. Owen felt that Nuri needed more briefing.

However, at this moment the servant came in to announce Miss Skinner's arrival.

'*Chère Madame!*' said Nuri, rising to kiss her hand.

'Mr Pasha!' said Miss Skinner, surprised but not discomfited.

'Call me Nuri,' said Zeinab's father, retaining her hand and leading her over to the divan.

Owen was glad that Paul was there. He had a feeling that things might be about to go wrong.

Fortunately, Zeinab appeared at this point, dressed as for a visit in discreet black, which owed, however, more to the fashion house than to Islamic tradition.

'I'm sorry I'm late,' she said. 'I've been at Samira's. Her favourite niece was being circumcised and it went on for ages—'

'Circumcised?' Miss Skinner's voice rose to a squeak. '*Female* circumcision?'

'Barbaric,' said Nuri. 'Reduces the pleasure enormously.'

'Miss Nuri, there are one or two things I would like to discuss—'

Paul somehow succeeded in detaching Miss Skinner from Nuri and leading her over to sit beside Zeinab, whose entrance, Owen thought, had not been entirely uncontrived.

He returned and sat down beside the disappointed Nuri.

'What an opportunity!' he said. 'The very man to tell us all the Khedive's secrets!'

'Alas, my friend,' said Nuri sadly, 'I am no longer one of his intimates.'

'Say not so! Why, only last week I was talking to Idris Bey and he said—'

'Did he?' said Nuri eagerly. 'Did he now?'

At the other end of the room Miss Skinner was deep in conversation with Zeinab. Owen shuddered to think what she might be hearing. Zeinab's knowledge of the life led by 'ordinary' Egyptians was sketchy but her imagination vivid.

Paul, meanwhile, had slid smoothly on to current politics and was now, thank goodness, giving Nuri the political background to Miss Skinner's visit.

'Antiquities? I'm sure I have some. Or can lay my hands on some if Miss Skinner wishes to buy—'

'No, no. It's the actual excavation she's interested in. But also the export of such treasures from Egypt.'

'An excellent thing. What good can they do here? Some clumsy peasant is sure to break them. Much better to sell them. If only,' said Nuri wistfully, 'I had an unopened pyramid or two on my estates!'

'Miss Skinner's position is, I think, a little different. She wishes to stop the export of antiquities from Egypt.'

'Stop!' cried Nuri, aghast. 'But why should she want to do that?'

'She feels, I believe, that Egypt's remarkable heritage should be preserved.'

'Oh quite,' said Nuri. 'Absolutely.'

He seemed, however, a little cast down.

'But, tell me, my friend,' he began again tentatively, 'exactly what business is it of hers? These treasures do after all belong to us.'

'I think she feels, *mon cher* Pasha, that they belong to the world.'

'Belong to the world?' said Nuri, stunned.

'In the sense that they are part of the heritage of us all.'

'Well, yes,' said Nuri. 'In that sense. As long as it's in that sense. Though I still don't see—'

There was a little silence. At the other end of the room Miss Skinner and Zeinab chattered happily away.

Nuri sniffed.

'In any case,' he said, 'heritage! Pooh! That is all in the past. We must look to the future. I was saying so to the Khedive only the other day. We were discussing, as it happens, the sale of a temple, complete with colossi—'

'I think,' said Paul, 'that would be the kind of thing she had in mind.'

'The sale was to the British Museum, of course.'

'A difficult balance of interests,' said Paul, smiling and shaking his head. 'Difficult for all of us.'

Nuri caught at his arm.

'And therefore, my friend, to be approached with circumspection. You will urge that, won't you? This could create such problems for us—'

'A few antiquities?'

'Not so few. Not these days. Now that the price of cotton is so low. Some of my colleagues are going in for it in a big way. Raquat Pasha was telling me that he had appointed a European agent. Sidki Narwas Pasha has a permanent arrangement with a German museum. Two or three are getting together. Even the Khedive—'

Owen listened with deepening gloom. They were all in it, the big Pashas, the Khedive, the museums. It was a national industry.

'We rely on it,' Nuri was saying with emphasis. 'Absolutely rely on it. You must do something, my friend.'

Across the room Zeinab and Miss Skinner were bringing their conversation to an end.

'Surely there is something you can do, *mon cher?*' said Nuri earnestly to Paul. 'Persuade her to take up other interests, perhaps?'

'Well, there is the Women Question—'

'Ah yes,' said Nuri thoughtfully.

'But more immediately,' said Paul, 'there are her archæo-logical interests. I am taking her down to Der el Bahari at the end of this week.'

'Are you? Are you, indeed?'

The conversation ended and the women rose together.

'You do see now, don't you, Pasha,' said Paul quietly, 'the importance of these political questions?'

'Oh, quite,' said Nuri. 'Oh, quite.'

'It would be very unfortunate if Miss Skinner were to get the wrong impression.'

'Don't worry,' said Nuri Pasha. 'I know exactly how to handle Miss Skinner.'

Owen stuck his head into the bar room.

'Trevelyan here?'

'No,' said someone. 'He left this morning. He's on his way to Der el Bahari by now.'

'With our blessings,' said someone else.

'There's a lot of money riding on it,' said Carmichael, from Customs.

'Why's that?' asked Owen, coming definitely into the room.

'It's that damned woman,' said someone, Jopling, from Finance. 'We've promised him free drinks for a month if he can keep her down there for a fortnight.'

'More if he can do it for longer.'

'It's the end of the year,' someone explained, 'the finan-cial year, that is. We're up to our eyeballs in work recon-ciling everything in sight. And then this damned woman comes along, poking her nose in.'

'I don't mind her poking her nose in,' said Jopling. 'It's having to take time off to answer her silly questions.'

'If she'd just read the Accounts,' said someone else, obvi-ously also from Finance, 'that would be fine. But she wants to go behind them, keeps asking what they mean.'

'As if they meant anything, other than just an end-of-year story to keep everybody happy.'

'So we promised Trevelyan he could have free drinks every evening if he'd only get her out of our hair.'

'It's worth it.'

'It certainly is,' said Owen. 'I'd have cut myself in if I'd known. *Wahid whisky-soda, min fadlak.*'

He collected the whisky-soda and sat down in a corner with Jopling and Carmichael.

'Has she been getting in your hair, too?' asked Carmichael.

'My God, Owen,' said Jopling, 'if she's been looking at *your* finances—!'

'Thank you, not yet. She's concentrating on the white-wash boys rather than the workers. It's the antiques export business,' he said to Carmichael.

'That? The export licence stuff?'

'She can forget that,' said Jopling. 'The Treasury people back in Town are all Free-Traders. Now that the Liberals are back in power. They won't hear of a licence.'

'I don't know where she stands on the licence business,' said Owen. 'From what I've gathered, it's more a question of whether to allow antiques to be exported at all.'

'She wants to ban that? Bloody hell, that *would* create a rumpus.'

'It would. It is already.'

Jopling regarded him curiously.

'How do you come to be involved? It's not really your line, is it?' Like many people, he was uncertain exactly what was the Mamur Zapt's line. 'More Carmichael's.'

'Enforcement,' said Carmichael. 'He's on the enforcement side.'

'Stopping the smuggling? Blimey, you've got a job on! Good luck, mate!'

He drained his glass. Carmichael ordered another round.

'That's not the only thing,' said Owen. He told them about the incident in the Ataba.

'Somebody tried to push her under a tram?' said Jopling. 'Wish I'd thought of that. Might have been cheaper than the beer.'

'No one did anything,' scoffed Carmichael. 'She's imagining things.'

'That's a bit like the conclusion I'm coming to,' said Owen.

Owen heard the water-carrier before he saw him. Even in the uproar of the Ataba-el-Khadra he heard the clanging of the little brass cups. They gave out a note as clear as a bell.

And there he was, the brass cups slung round his neck in front of him, on his back a resplendent brass urn and, lower down, dangling from his waist, two black bulging water-skins.

In the richer parts of the city the water-sellers sometimes wore the old national dress; in the poorer, they dressed in rags. This one compromised, wearing shirt-style tunic on top, rags below, so that it didn't matter when he walked into the Nile to replenish his skins.

As he moved through the crowd, slowly because of his burden, he gave the traditional cry: 'May God compensate me!'

Owen caught his eye and the man moved towards him.

'Compensation is at hand, brother!' he said.

The man smiled, produced a cup, bent deftly and a cool, clear spurt of water leaped over his shoulder and into the cup without spilling a drop.

'And there is yet more compensation if you can tell me what I seek to know.'

He took the cup and sipped it.

'If I know, then I will tell you,' said the man.

'Two days ago,' said Owen, 'you were at this spot at this

time and you were able to help a lady when she fell.'

The water-seller looked at him curiously.

'Yes,' he said, 'I remember the lady.'

'What else do you remember?' asked Owen. 'Did you see her fall?'

'I saw her fall and I saw her hit the tram and I thought: God protect her! And I think He did, for when I got to her she was lying beside the tram, hurt, I think, but not broken.'

'This is good water,' said Owen. 'Give me some more.'

The man bent again and refilled the cup.

'She hit the tram,' said Owen. 'The tram did not hit her?'

The water-carrier made a gesture with his hand.

'Are they not the same?'

'No,' said Owen, 'for you speak as if the tram might not have hit her had she not herself moved.'

'She was falling,' said the water-carrier. 'She fell towards the tram.'

'And hit its side?'

'Yes. High up. Which is fortunate, I think, as it knocked her away, so that she did not fall beneath the wheels.'

'She must, then, have been standing close to it?'

The water-carrier nodded.

'Yes, effendi, in the street, quite close to its path.'

'But not actually in its path?'

'No, not in its path.'

Owen handed the cup back.

'You speak as if you saw all clearly,' he said.

The water-carrier bowed his head.

'I did see all clearly. I was standing not far from her and there was no one between us.'

'Then perhaps,' said Owen, 'you can tell me how she came to fall?'

The water-carrier hesitated.

'I should be able to,' he said, 'but—'

'Did she stumble?'

'She stumbled, yes. But that was after—'

'Yes?'

The water-carrier hesitated for a long time and then looked Owen straight in the eye.

'After she was pushed,' he said.

CHAPTER 3

'Hamidullah,' said Owen, 'this is a big thing that you have said.'

He had taken the water-carrier over to the pavement by the arabeah stand and they were sitting down on the kerb. A yard or two away the cab-horses munched the green fodder spread for them in the gutter.

'I know,' said Hamidullah, 'and it was not said lightly.'

'Then say it again.'

'She was pushed,' said Hamidullah. 'I saw it with my own eyes.'

'Tell me what you saw.'

'I saw her coming my way. And I said: "Hamidullah, that lady is not for you. She will not want your water." For she was a splendid lady and had a mighty hat. I kept my eye on her, though, for she was coming in my direction and I did not wish to brush against her with my bags lest her fine dress be besmirched. And as she came towards me—'

The water-carrier stopped and looked bewildered.

'What as she came towards you?'

The water-carrier hesitated.

'I would not say it if I had not seen it. A hand reached out and thrust at her.'

'Where did it touch her?'

Hamidullah reached up under his urn and touched himself in the small of the back.

'Here,' he said. 'Right here. I was amazed. I could not believe my eyes.'

'It was a heavy push?'

'Effendi, it must have been a heavy push to make her fall like that. One moment she was walking along mightily. Like this.' This water-carrier stuck his nose in the air and mimicked marching. 'The next, she had fallen like this.'

The water-carrier sprawled along the pavement.

'It was not then, oh, a little push such as one gives when one is impatient and someone is in the way?'

'Oh no, effendi. One should not give a push, even a little one, for that is lacking in courtesy. But this was not a little push. It was . . . I stood amazed!'

'You see, Hamidullah, if it was not a little push, such as one might give in passing if one is lacking in courtesy, but a big push, then someone must have meant to injure the lady.'

'Well, yes, effendi. That is why I stood amazed. For this was not—not discourtesy, effendi, this was—well, wrong!'

Hamidullah looked at him wide-eyed, still shocked.

Over his shoulder Owen could hear the horses munching and there, its head swaying incongruously above the roofs of the arabeahs, a camel was approaching with another load of forage.

Owen restrained an urge to pat the water-carrier.

'It *was* wrong, Hamidullah,' he said solemnly, 'and therefore I have one more thing to ask you. You saw the hand; did you see the man?'

'No, effendi.'

'You saw the hand,' said Owen. 'Did you not see to whom it belonged?'

'There were people standing. The lady stepped out to go round them. And then, as I watched, a hand reached out from among the people and gave her a push, a fierce push, as she went past. I saw only the hand.'

'No face, no clothes?'

Hamidullah shook his head.

'There were people in the way. I saw only the hand.'

'The hand must have been attached to an arm; tell me
about the arm.'

'I—I do not remember.'

'How was it clothed? In a sleeve like mine or a sleeve like
yours?'

'Like mine, effendi.'

'The colour?'

'I do not remember.'

'Blue? White?'

Hamidullah hesitated.

'Blue, I think, effendi.'

'A fellah's?'

'I—I think so, effendi. Effendi, I am sorry. I did not see.
It all happened so quickly.'

Owen could get no more out of him. A hand in the crowd
he had seen: but that had been all he had seen.

'And that's not enough,' said Garvin, the Commandant of
the Cairo Police.

'Enough to constitute an assault, surely,' objected
McPhee, the Deputy Commandant.

They were sitting in McPhee's office. Owen had gone on
to see him the moment he got back to the Bab-el-Khalk
and McPhee, who took seriously any attack on a European,
had asked Garvin to come in and join them.

'Technically, perhaps,' said Garvin. 'But doesn't it
depend on the severity of the push?'

'It was a violent push,' said Owen. 'Both Miss Skinner
and Hamidullah said so.'

'A well-to-do lady, genteel, in Cairo for the first time?
Not used to Cairo crowds? Any push would probably seem
violent to her.'

'Hamidullah thought so too.'

'Well,' said Garvin, who had been twenty years in Egypt
and knew his Cairenes, particularly the poorer ones, 'isn't

the same likely to be true of him? *Any* push, given that it was to a Sitt, would seem violent to them.'

'It was violent enough to make her fall over,' Owen pointed out.

'She was pushed, and she fell over. The two don't have to be connected. Maybe she was just caught off balance.'

'The tram is what bothers me,' said McPhee.

'Nothing to do with it. It just happened to be passing at the time. That's all.'

McPhee was unconvinced.

'I'm not happy about it,' he said. 'Egyptians are not like that. They don't go round pushing people. They're like Hamidullah. They'd be shocked at anybody pushing a lady.'

'A crowd,' said Garvin. 'Somebody standing in the way?'

McPhee shook his head.

'They'd go round them.'

'In any case,' said Owen, 'it wasn't like that. Not according to Hamidullah. He says she was the one who was going round. She stepped out to pass and then a hand came out and pushed her.'

'That's the bit I find—' said McPhee.

'A hand in the crowd!' said Garvin. 'That's all. That's not much to go on, is it? Not much to ask the Parquet to build a case on.'

'We've got to do something about it,' said McPhee. 'We can't just leave it. If only in the interests of the lady's future protection.'

Garvin was silent for a moment, turning things over.

'Is that a factor, though?'

'Of course it is!' said McPhee. 'Really—!'

'Yes, but is it?' Garvin insisted. He turned to Owen. 'How long did you say she'd been in the country?'

'Ten days.'

'Hardly long enough to earn yourself an enemy, is it? And she's not likely to have brought one with her!'

'What are you saying?'

'I'm just wondering whether the attack was directed against her personally.'

'She was the one who was attacked, wasn't she?' said McPhee belligerently.

'Yes, but not because she was Miss Skinner.'

'Why, then?'

'Because she was something else. A European—or seemed so to them. Or—how about this?—a European woman.'

'Some fanatic?'

'Offended because she was improperly dressed. Wasn't wearing a veil.'

'This is Cairo,' Owen objected. 'Surely they're used to European women?'

'Perhaps whoever pushed her was not.'

'Or some brand of Nationalist. Offended, anyway.'

There was a little silence.

'It has to be something like that, doesn't it?' asked Garvin. 'It couldn't really be because of anything personal to Miss Skinner. She's not been here long enough for that.'

Owen thought about it.

'You could be right,' he said slowly.

'And if I am,' said Garvin, 'we don't have to worry about protecting her. It's a one-off and won't be repeated.'

'It had better not be,' said Owen. 'Her uncle could be the next President of the United States.'

McPhee went over to the window and poured himself some water from the earthenware pot standing there to cool.

'It mightn't be a bad idea if someone spoke to her. Tipped her off about the veil.'

'Owen can do that.'

'No, I can't. She's not in town any longer.'

'Where is she?'

'Der el Bahari.'

'Der el Bahari? All the better. She'll be out of harm's way there.'

But Miss Skinner would return. And when she returned she would want to know what he had done about that antiquities business. He decided to start at the Museum.

An under-keeper, harassed-looking, intercepted him at the door.

'We're moving the cow,' he said.

'Cow?'

'You know. Of course you know.'

Owen racked his brain.

'The Cow of Hathor,' said the under-keeper impatiently.

The name tickled his memory.

'Haven't I read something about it?'

'Eighteen months ago. The newspapers were full of it.'

'I remember! It was found—found in some temple—'

'Menthu Hetep.'

'—and brought here. There was a lot of fuss about it.'

'Rightly so,' said the under-keeper huffily. 'It's one of the best things we've got.'

Some workmen walked backwards into the foyer pulling on ropes as if they were a tug-of-war team.

'Steady!' cried the under-keeper. 'Steady!'

Behind them glided a podium on which stood a beautifully formed cow, carved out of limestone and painted reddish-brown with black spots. On its head it wore a hat.

'A lunar disk,' corrected the under-keeper, 'with two feathers. It's the normal head-dress of Hathor.'

'I see. But what—?'

Below the head was the carved form of a man.

'He's the king grown up,' said the under-keeper. 'This is him as a boy.'

At the other end of the cow, sucking milk from its udders, was a small boy. There was an intimacy and humanity about the composition unusual in Egyptian statuary.

'Nice, isn't it?' said the under-keeper affectionately.

The tug-of-war team disappeared down a corridor and the cow slid after it, hotly pursued by agitated Museum officials in tarbooshes.

'Now what was it you wanted? The Despatch Room?'

He led Owen beneath the jaws of some twenty-foot-high colossi, past a row of intimidatingly lifelike painted statues of Pharaohs and into a room in which were several half-open sarcophagi and various mummies in different degrees of undress.

The under-keeper stopped for a moment, startled, but then recovered, strode firmly across the room and moved a brightly gilt sarcophagus lid which was leaning against the wall.

'You never know what to do with these damned things,' he said.

Behind the lid was a door which led down some steps into a basement. Some men were bending over packing cases and a clerk was standing by with what looked like an invoice in his hand.

'Hello, Lucas,' said the under-keeper, 'we've come to see what you do about exports.'

'You've come at the right time,' said the clerk, glancing at the invoice. 'Would you like to do some valuing while you're here?'

The clerk, like most of the clerks in Cairo, was a Copt and had the round and slightly flattened face of some of the statues upstairs. The Copts were the original people of Egypt; the Arabs had come later.

'What have you got for me?' asked the under-keeper.

Lucas indicated the packing cases.

'How many? Three? Oh, that won't take long.'

He bent over one of the cases and looked at the label.

'Brownlow,' he said, 'Captain Brownlow. One of the boys going home on leave.'

He began to take things out of the case.

'One set of Canopic jars, eighteenth-century, good condition, fifteen hundred piastres; one jar, large, Twenty-
Third Dynasty, slightly chipped, seven hundred piastres;
one kursi table, small, twelve hundred piastres; four
mummy-bead necklaces—all the girlfriends, I expect, no,
he could have sisters, where was I, Lucas—?'

'Necklaces,' said the clerk, pencil busy.

'Necklaces, oh, say two hundred each. Six clay ushapti
images, six hundred piastres, wait a minute, these look like
ours—' the Museum had an excellent Salle de Vente—
'shows he's got good taste, anyway; ornamental scarabs,
good God, how many? Say three hundred piastres—'

He went on to the next box. The clerk checked the items
and entered a value for each.

'Quick,' said Owen.

'It looks casual, I dare say,' said the under-keeper defensively, 'but when you've done hundreds of them and there's
nothing out of the ordinary, you can do it pretty fast.'

'What happens when there is something out of the
ordinary?'

'I check it in the catalogues, see the latest prices. Usually
there's something fairly similar. Of course, if you get something like the Cow, what do you do? Pluck a figure out of
the air, I suppose. One bust of Nefertiti, oh, a million, say?
Pounds, not piastres. One mummy, Tutankhamen, two
million? What am I bid for this Pyramid?'

Owen laughed. 'It gets impossible, doesn't it?'

'Things like that ought to be treated differently. There
ought to be a permit system or something.'

'Yes. I've heard that argument.'

'The trouble is that whatever value you put on it, they've
only got to pay 2.5% tax.'

'On a million . . . ?'

The under-keeper gave a quick, dismissive shrug.

'Yes, but it doesn't really work like that. If it's something
really special—like the Cow, say,—what stops it from being

sold abroad is the publicity. It's not so much publicity in
the country, though we do what we can—remember all
that stuff about the Cow?—it's more what goes on outside
the country. Say what you like about the Consul General,
but he's usually sensitive on such matters, especially the
new one.'

'Yes, there's a lot of interest in our export of antiquities
just now,' said Owen with feeling.

'All it does, though,' said the under-keeper with equal
feeling, 'is to encourage them to by-pass the ordinary procedures. They pick up something, keep quiet about it, and
smuggle it out of the country without us hearing anything
about it.'

'How do they do that?'

'I don't know,' said the under-keeper. 'You'll have to talk
to the Customs people at Alexandria about that.'

The workmen were busy repacking the cases. As each
one was finished, a senior workman came forward and
nailed the lid back on. The clerk examined it carefully and
then applied a seal.

'We do what we can,' said the under-keeper.

'What happens after this?'

'The case gets taken away and sent to Alexandria. One
copy of our valuation goes with the case. Another is sent to
the Mudir of Customs at Alexandria. We keep a third.'

'So a copy travels with the case?'

'Yes, and is matched up against the one we send direct
to the Mudir.'

'What happens if there is no valuation statement?'

'You'd better ask the Mudir.'

On the way out they went by a different route so that
the under-keeper could check that the Cow was safely in
position.

'One of our most popular exhibits,' said the under-keeper
fondly.

Owen lingered to look.

'Nice, isn't it? One of the best things we've ever had from Der el Bahari.'

'Why don't we got to Alexandria for a couple of days?' suggested Owen.

'What for?' asked Zeinab.

'The sea air. Escape from the heat.'

'Half of Cairo will be doing that,' said Zeinab. 'Not me.'

'Oh, come on. I thought I'd take a look at the Customs arrangements down there.'

'Customs arrangements?' said Zeinab incredulously. 'Well, that does sound tempting!'

'We could,' said Owen, who had anticipated this response and done his homework, 'go to the Zizinia in the evening. They're doing *I Maestri Cantori di Norimberga*, which we've not seen yet. And we might be able to fit in *La Bohème* as well.'

'That's different,' said Zeinab.

And so two mornings later Owen arrived at the office of the Directeur Local des Douanes d'Alexandrie.

'But, my dear fellow,' cried the Mudir of Customs, 'why did you not come on a donkey?'

Why not, indeed? To get to the Customs House he had been obliged to walk along nearly two miles of quays. The quays were paved and the stone was so hot that even with shoes on Owen stepped gingerly. The sea to his left reflected the sunlight so dazzlingly that he was almost blinded; and immediately to his right had rumbled an almost continuous train of mule carts which threw up such a cloud of dust that by the time he arrived at the Customs House his tarboosh was quite white.

The Mudir tut-tutted and wiped him down and ordered a lemonade.

'Now, my dear chap,' he said, 'what is it this time? Hashish, guns or dirty postcards?'

'Antiquities.'

'Antiquities?' The Mudir was surprised. 'But they're straightforward. Relatively!' he added hurriedly.

'All the same . . .'

The Mudir led him into a long shed. There was a large door at one end, beyond which Owen could see a queue of waiting vehicles.

'Goods Arrival,' said the Mudir.

Porters were bringing packing cases in through the door in a steady stream. They carried the cases high up on their shoulders, one man to a case, irrespective, it seemed, of the dimensions of the case. As each one came through the door, an official seized him, turned him round, read the label on the case and directed him to one or other part of the shed.

Sometimes the porters came clutching documents in their hands. Usually, however, the paperwork was handled separately by an effendi, be-suited and be-tarbooshed, who fussed around chivvying the porters and generally taking responsibility for the consignment.

'They're the Agency people,' said the Mudir. 'We get to know them quite well.'

'What do they do?' asked Owen.

'Well, suppose you had brought some antiquities and you wanted to send them back to England: you could do it yourself or you could ask an Agency to handle it for you. Most people use an Agency. It saves a lot of work. You see, if it's antiquities you have to send them to the Museum to be valued—'

'Yes,' said Owen. 'I know about that.'

'You do? Well, you can see it's much simpler if an Agency does it all for you. They pick up the antiquities, pack them, send them to the Museum, collect them, despatch them to Alexandria and see them through the Customs here. Much simpler.'

Among the effendis was a young woman in a long green coat.

'Is she an Agency person, too?'

The Mudir frowned.

'I wouldn't have thought so.'

The woman seemed, however, to be taking responsibility for a consignment. She accosted a Sous-Inspecteur, led him over to a small pile of cases and gave him some papers.

'It's unusual,' said the Mudir. 'I've never known—'

It was unusual for a woman to be engaged in business of any kind, much less in public, unless she was the lowest of the low, an orange-seller in a market, say. But this woman was well dressed and European, or if not European, a Levantine of some sort.

'I think I've seen her before, though,' said the Mudir.

The Sous-Inspecteur was counting the cases. The woman took one of the documents back from him and went off with a look of determination. The Sous-Inspecteur began scrutinizing the cases.

'Is he going to open them?' asked Owen.

'That depends. If the paperwork is in order he might not. You know about the paperwork? The Museum sends us a copy of its valuation direct. The other copy goes with the case. The copies don't come together again until the case gets here, so there is no possibility of tampering with the list.'

'Adding something?'

'Altering a value, perhaps.'

'Perhaps something could be added to the case but not to the list?'

'The Mudir shook his head.

'Unlikely,' he said. 'The cases are sealed at the Museum.'

'Still—'

The Sous-Inspecteur pounced on a case and began opening it.

'Like to have a look?' asked the Mudir. He took Owen by the arm and led him across to the Sous-Inspecteur. 'Why that one?' he asked.

'The seal looks as if it could have been tampered with,' said the Sous-Inspecteur.

'That's the first thing we check,' explained the Mudir. 'Of course, if you're clever, it's always possible to open the case without breaking the seal.'

'You'd have to be very clever, though, to do it without leaving a mark,' said the Sous-Inspecteur. 'We look for that, too.'

He began to unpack the case carefully, checking each item against the list: rather beautiful Canopic jars and two delicate figurines.

'Seems all right,' said the Sous-Inspecteur, signalling to a workman to come and put the lid back on. As it was hammered into a position he bent over the case and marked it carefully.

'Two marks,' said the Mudir. 'One to show it's been passed, the other to show it's been opened.'

'What's this one?' said the Sous-Inspecteur, pointing to a case which stood a little apart from the others.

The workman shook his head.

'I'll have a look at it.'

It was a large, flat case, taller than the others but less wide. The workman prised one side off. As it came away it revealed a stone figure carefully padded with straw and wrapped in thick folds of green beige. The Sous-Inspecteur pulled the cloth away. The figure was that of a marvellously-carved dog-headed ape.

'What's the value?' said the Sous-Inspecteur to himself, consulting his list. 'Thirty thousand piastres? Is that all? Still, it's what the Museum says. Now, two and a half per cent of thirty thousand—'

'Seven hundred and fifty piastres,' said Owen. 'Seventy-five pounds. It doesn't seem much.'

'What are you doing with my Thoth?' said a cool voice beside him.

It was the girl in the green coat.

'Is it yours?' said the Sous-Inspecteur. 'It was a bit apart from the others.'

'I didn't see it. I've been looking all over the place for it. I thought for a moment they must have left it behind. Well,' she said to Owen, 'what do you think of it?'

'Very fine,' he said genuinely.

'It is, isn't it?' she said, stroking its ears. 'I shall be sorry to part with this one.'

'Aren't you parting with it a little too cheaply?'

She looked startled.

'I don't think so,' she said. 'I hope not.'

'Thirty thousand piastres?'

'It's the going price. We've got a shop in Milan.'

Ah. Not, probably, Levantine, then. One of the enormous colony of Italians in Alexandria.

'That's pretty low, surely, for an original statuette of this quality?'

'I don't know about this quality, but it would be pretty low, certainly, for an original statuette. If it were one.'

'It's—it's not genuine?'

'It's perfectly genuine,' said the girl, rather put out. 'It just happens to be an imitation.'

Feeling rather foolish, Owen bent over the ape-god and examined it.

'It's not always easy to tell,' the girl said, taking pity on him. 'If it's well done, often the only way you know is by the buff of the stone.'

She took his hand and placed his fingers on the ape-god's backside.

'You see? Too smooth, too regular. Our tools are better than theirs. There are always roughnesses in an original.'

She released his hand and stood up with a laugh.

'So you see,' she said, 'thirty thousand piastres is not unreasonable.'

'It's a very good imitation.'

'We deal in quality,' said the girl.

'*Ta'ib*,' said the Sous-Inspecteur. 'It is well.' The work-man came forward and replaced the side on the box.

'What would you like to see now?' asked the Mudir. 'The paperwork? Or shall I tell you about Security?'

Afterwards, they went back to the Mudir's office for coffee. As Owen raised his cup to his mouth, he caught the slight smell of perfume on his hand.

The Opera House was small and gracious, the audience large and enthusiastic. But largely Italian: and therefore not at all sure of *The Mastersingers*, which was their first experience of Wagner.

Zeinab wasn't sure either. When she went to the opera she always identified strongly with the heroines but in this case felt there was not a lot to identify with.

'She is too passive,' she complained to Owen at the interval.

Passive was something Zeinab was not. She had all the emotional volatility—and some of the dramatic self-centredness—of an operatic diva.

'The men have all the best parts,' she said darkly. 'I am not sure I like this Wagner. He is too cold, too stiff. Like an Englishman.'

Taking this personally, Owen pointed out that he was Welsh.

'Deceptive, as always,' said Zeinab, tucking her arm beneath his.

'Oh, hallo!'

It was Carmichael, from Customs, recognizing Owen but uncertain how to take his lady, obviously on intimate terms with him but not, surely—an Arab?—his wife.

'Miss Al Nuri,' said Owen.

'Oh, hallo!' said Carmichael awkwardly. It was very rarely that one met an Egyptian woman, even in relatively westernized contexts such as the opera. One did not often meet women at all—the Mediterranean peoples were very jealous of their women—but Egyptians, never.

The Mamur Zapt, he supposed, was different.

Zeinab, enjoying his discomfort, flashed her eyes at him over her veil. Carmichael went pink.

'Up for a visit?' he said hurriedly to Owen.

'Taking a look at Customs.'

'Oh, you'll find that very interesting,' said Carmichael enthusiastically. 'Hamdi Pasha runs a tight ship. One of Chitty Bey's men.'

Chitty Bey, the remarkable man who had set up the Customs Administration in its present form, was a legend in the land.

'He certainly seemed on top of things,' said Owen.

A bell rang and they went back into the cream and gilt splendour of the auditorium, with its enclosed harem boxes to left and right.

The opera came to an end with its last long bit which Owen dismissed as merely praise of the Fatherland. The audience, too, was uncertain how to take it. At last some of them made up their minds to reinterpret it in terms of Egyptian nationhood and applauded vigorously.

'Bloody Nationalists!' said Carmichael, pink again. 'Spoil everything!'

They emerged into the foyer.

'Want a lift?'

There was a huge rush for arabeahs as everyone came out of the theatre and they were glad to share the one he had previously booked.

As they drove round the bay they passed the Customs area.

'Tight ship,' said Carmichael with satisfaction. 'Not the way it used to be. See that house?' He jerked his thumb at a sumptuous villa set deep in magnificent shrubs and trees. 'Built by the chap in charge of valuing the cotton piece goods. Before Chitty Bey's time, of course. Manchester House, we call it.'

'Perhaps there's one like it for antiquities,' said Owen.

There was a message from Garvin waiting for him at the hotel. It said: '*Get down to Der el Bahari quick. Something's happened to Miss Skinner.*'

CHAPTER 4

Getting down to Der al Bahari was not as straightforward as might appear. It was, to start with, over four hundred miles from Cairo and the last part of the journey would have to be by mule. The first part, however, need not be made by boat, as Miss Skinner had done. It could be covered by train; more particularly, in the splendid new Wagons-Lits which had just come into service.

Owen boarded the train just before it departed and was relieved to see that no one was occupying the other berth. He opened the window and once the train began to move there was a pleasantly cooling draught. He would have to shut it later on when it became dark, not just because of the thieves but because of the mosquitoes. The windows were tinted to reduce the glare but anyway at this point in the day, late in the afternoon, the sun was beginning to soften.

He sat for some time watching the fields go by with the fellahin at work in them coaxing the water along the furrows. Every so often there was a high mudbank behind which was a canal and on this high ground there was frequently someone standing; a boy with a buffalo, a woman with a water-jar, Biblical shepherds with their flocks.

After a while, though, the fields gave way to desert and the buffalo to the occasional camel. He got up and went along to the club car for a drink and then, since there were too many people smoking, carried the drink on through to the restaurant-car.

It was not yet time for dinner and the place was deserted except for a young Egyptian, Moslem and therefore non-smoking and non-drinking, sitting alone at a table.

'Mahmoud!'

The young man sprang up.

'*Cher ami!*'

They embraced, Arab-style.

'But what are you doing here?'

'I'm on my way to Luxor,' said Owen, 'and then to Der el Bahari. Something's happened to a woman there.'

'Der el Bahari? But this is extraordinary! I am on my way to Der el Bahari, too. Though not for the same reason. Tell me about this woman.'

He listened engrossed.

'It sounds as if it may be coming our way,' he said.

Mahmoud el Zaki was a member of the Parquet, the Department of Prosecutions of the Ministry of Justice. The legal system in Egypt followed French rather than English tradition. The law itself was based upon the Code Napoléon and investigation of a potential crime was the responsibility not of the police, as in England, but of an independent prosecution service, as in France.

When a potential crime was reported, the Parquet would appoint an officer to the case, a lawyer, like Mahmoud, who would assume responsibility not just for the investigation but also for bringing the case to the courts. He would conduct the case in the court, acting as what in England would be known as prosecuting counsel.

Owen had worked with Mahmoud before and the two got on very well. The young Egyptian had the political skill to operate in a country where the Government was not the Government, where there were four competing systems of jurisdiction and criminals could dodge easily between them, and where religious and ethnic differences continually threatened to pervert the frail legal process. Mahmoud was, not surprisingly, one of the Parquet's rising stars.

But what was he doing here?

'I thought you kept to Cairo?'

Mahmoud grimaced.

'Well, it's hot,' he said. 'It's nice to get out of the city.'

'It's a lot hotter in Der el Bahari.'

'That's probably why they're sending me there!' said Mahmoud. 'The courts are in recess for the summer and they're fed up of me hanging about the office!'

'Oh yes!'

'Several people are away on holiday,' Mahmoud explained, 'so they've sent me down to handle this one.'

'What is this one?'

'It's an industrial case, actually. A workman. Killed in an accident.'

'I didn't know you got involved in those?'

'We don't, usually. But this one is different. It's the second one in the same place.'

'Oh, I see. Criminal neglect on the part of the employer. Something like that?'

Mahmoud nodded.

'Something like that.'

The waiters began to serve dinner. Owen chose *ful Sudani* for the soup. Mahmoud went for *bouillon*.

'I didn't know there was any industry at Der el Bahari,' said Owen. 'Apart from the fabrication of antiquities, of course.'

'It's an excavation site.'

'An excavation?' said Owen, sitting up.

'You think it might have something to do with your case?'

'Two deaths? And then Miss Skinner? I'm beginning to wonder.'

*

'Really, Captain Owen,' said Miss Skinner calmly, 'I don't think there was any need for you to come all this way. It was just a little accident and, fortunately, not at all serious.'

'You spoke of an attack,' said Paul quietly.

'Did I? Well, an attack of nerves, perhaps. Or maybe it was the bats. It was all very confusing. But an attack? Oh dear no. A mishap, which I may well have brought upon myself.'

'It was a damned stupid thing to do,' said Parker harshly. He was the tall, heavy-set American who was directing excavations on the site.

'Perhaps it was,' said Miss Skinner, looking at him coolly. 'Perhaps it was.'

'Certainly there was no need to bring anybody down from Cairo,' said Parker. 'Complete waste of time. And money.'

'Mr Trevelyan is usually a pretty good judge of the public interest,' said Owen.

'It's not the public's time and money that I'm talking about. It's mine.'

Parker stood up abruptly, walked out from under the awning and shouted to some workmen who were sitting quietly in the shadow cast by the wall of the temple. Two of them stood up and hurried away.

'Isn't it time to stop for the day?' asked Mahmoud.

They had arrived at Der el Bahari in the late afternoon. The shadows were already creeping out from the cliff. This far south, though, the sun retained its heat till late.

'I'm the judge of that,' said Parker.

'I was thinking of the legal limits,' said Mahmoud.

'What damned business is it of yours?' asked Parker.

'The hours of work will be one of the things I'll be looking at,' said Mahmoud.

Parker turned and faced him.

'Oh, you will, will you?' he said furiously. 'Well, who the hell are you?'

'Mahmoud el Zaki. Department of Prosecutions, Ministry of Justice.'

'Really, Mr Trevelyan,' began Miss Skinner, 'you shouldn't have gone to all this trouble—'

'Two of them!' said Parker disgustedly. 'Two! They send two people down from Cairo just because of a crazy woman! Haven't you got anything to do? You haven't, I suppose.'

'I am afraid you're under a misapprehension, Mr Parker,' said Mahmoud quietly. 'I am not investigating, at present, the circumstances in which Miss Skinner was attacked. I am investigating, for the Department of Prosecutions, the circumstances in which two workmen have died.'

'Oh, oh!' said Miss Skinner, putting her hand over her mouth. 'Two!'

Parker now was giving Mahmoud his full attention.

'Those were accidents,' he said. 'It happens sometimes when you're digging. Sites are dangerous places.'

'I shall be looking at the circumstances in which the accidents took place,' said Mahmoud, 'in order to determine whether there are any questions of criminal liability.'

'I'm an American,' said Parker. 'You can't get me with Egyptian law.'

Owen saw Mahmoud's face harden.

'It is true,' the Egyptian admitted softly, 'that any prosecution would have to be within the terms of the Capitulations procedure.'

'Well, then—'

'However, that is true only of formal prosecution. There are other things I could recommend. Such as withdrawing your licence to excavate.'

Parker turned purple.

'You'd better not!' he said. 'There are big people behind this. We're putting real money into this goddamned country and we're not going to be messed around by clerks from Cairo. As you will damned soon find!'

Mahmoud rose to his feet.

'Meanwhile,' he said quietly, 'I shall carry on with my investigations.'

He walked over to the circle of workmen, crouched down and began to talk to them.

Parker watched him in fury for a few moments, then turned on his heel and strode away.

'My!' said Miss Skinner. 'My!'

She sat for a while turning things over in her mind. Then she looked up.

'You know,' she said, 'I think I'm glad on the whole that you *did* send for Captain Owen. Two workmen? Two? Yes,' she said thoughtfully, looking at Paul. 'Yes, you were quite right.'

Owen woke early, as he did every morning, stood up at once and walked out from under the awning. Over to the east, across the Plain of Thebes, the sun was rising in a great ball of red and orange. The plain, though, was still covered in shadows and it was cold enough, without a jacket, to make him shiver.

There was a pump not far away with a few workmen clustered round it, washing their faces. They used the water sparingly, letting it trickle into their hands and then spreading it over face, arms and upper body. He went across and joined them, then half filled a mug and began to shave.

One of the men took the mug silently, walked over to the fire, picked up the kettle and topped up the mug with hot water. Owen thanked him, they fell into conversation and it was natural to follow him afterwards and join the ring drinking black tea around the fire.

The sun was just beginning now to touch the tops of the cliffs above the camp. They rose in a steep wall to cut off the plain from the Sahara and at their foot, cut into the rock, was the incredible temple of Queen Hatshepsut, with its three great terraces, one behind the other, its marvellous double colonnades, open to the light, open to the eyes of men from miles around, but sloping back into the darkness of the cliffs and the holiest of holies.

'*C'est magnifique*,' said Paul, suddenly appearing beside him, '*mais ce n'est pas* the particular one they're working on.'

'Oh? What one are they working on?'

'That one,' said Paul, pointing along the cliffs to where a second temple nestled into the rock. It was smaller than the Hatshepsut temple and sadly ruined.

'And therefore,' said Paul, 'neglected until about five years ago, when Naville began his excavations. You've met Naville? No? Well, you should. An interesting man and found some interesting things: the Cow of Hathor, for instance. You remember the Cow of Hathor? There was a lot about it in the papers—'

'Saw it last week,' said Owen. 'They were moving it.'

'Not part of the general exodus, I hope?'

'No, no. Just from one part of the Museum to the other.'

'I would hate to lose that,' said Paul. 'It might almost induce me to join forces with Miss Skinner.'

'And it was over there, was it,' asked Owen, looking across at the second temple, 'that it happened?'

'It' according to Miss Skinner last night had been a simple fall. She had gone back alone one evening after excavation had finished for the day—'oh, in the quiet, you know. I just wanted to take a quiet look, when there were no workmen fidgeting around'—and had fallen into a subterranean chamber.

'My own fault,' Miss Skinner had said.

'Yes,' Parker had said heavily, 'it was. You ought to know better. Damned unprofessional.'

'There was a thing I wished to check on.'

'Well, just check on it in the daytime in future,' Parker had said.

'How did you come to fall, Miss Skinner?' Owen had asked.

'Oh. I don't know. The hole was there for me to see, wasn't it? And I had a torch. I must have been looking at something else, I suppose.'

She had lain there for the rest of the night. It was not until the morning that her absence had been discovered. And it was not until late the following day that her cries had been heard. They might not have been heard then had not Parker, angry at yet more time being lost, ordered some of his men back to work.

'However,' said Miss Skinner briskly, 'no bones broken. And there was no other damage apart from that to my self-esteem. Except, of course, that poor Mr Trevelyan was most frightfully worried.'

She laughed and patted Paul playfully on the knee. 'My faithful Achates,' she said.

Paul had smiled dutifully but said nothing.

This morning he was still saying nothing.

'Take a look at it first,' he said. 'We can talk later.'

They were going over, as soon as it became light, to take a look at the scene of the incident. Already the workmen were beginning to make their way out of the camp.

'Breakfast!' called Miss Skinner. 'Breakfast is served!'

They joined her under the awning, where a bare wooden trestle table had been set up. The camp cook, rising nobly and convinced that no European ate anything other than eggs for breakfast, produced some well fried ones, together, however, with coffee, which Parker apparently insisted on.

Parker himself was nowhere to be seen. He was already closeted with Mahmoud.

'Where's Naville?' asked Owen. 'Didn't you say he was conducting the excavation?'

'No, no. He finished two years ago. There was a gap and then Parker applied for the licence.'

'Thinking that where the pickings had been so good, there might be more,' said Miss Skinner.

'Another Cow?'

'A calf at least.'

Already the heat was rising up from the ground and bouncing back from the cliffs. This far south it was several degrees hotter than in Cairo and in the vast amphitheatre of rock it was hotter still. As they walked across to the second temple Owen could now see why the workmen had been glad to leave so early.

In the open court of the temple they stopped at the entrance to a sloping passage extending down below the pavement. A modern door had been fitted—'to keep out jay-walkers,' said Miss Skinner—but was standing open.

Inside was a rocky tunnel the height and width of a man, except that the men were smaller in those days and Owen had to stoop. It ran steeply downwards for over a hundred metres and then came out into a large room made of blocks of granite, extremely well joined, as they saw in the light of the torches. Two other tunnels ran out of the room.

'That one,' said Miss Skinner, pointing, 'goes down to the sanctuary. That's where they're working at the moment. This one, here, is the one I went down.'

'Not where they were working?'

'I had been there. On my way back I thought I'd try this one.'

The second tunnel was just as well made as the one they had walked down previously, except that it was, perhaps, a trifle smaller. The roof was vaulted and the floor, though bare rock, carefully smoothed.

Paul, in front, stopped.

'The scene of the crime,' said Miss Skinner.

'Crime?' said Owen.

'Accident,' said Miss Skinner.

The hole was not in front, as Owen had supposed, but at the side, in the wall. A cold, dusty smell came out of the opening.

Paul shone his torch inside.

'It's a drop, as you can see.'

'How far?'

'Five feet,' said Miss Skinner. 'I could see over it, standing on tiptoe. But I couldn't get up. There was nothing to stand on. Except mummies, of course, and they kept collapsing.'

'Mummies?'

Paul shone his torch.

'There are dozens down there.'

'They are mainly cats and dogs,' said Miss Skinner. 'Although there are some crocodiles.'

'You tried standing on them?'

'It was all I could find. The torch had, of course, gone out.'

'How did you know—?'

'I could feel them. The different animals are quite distinctive, even in the dark. I was down there, of course, for some time.'

In the torchlight Owen could see the mummies, lots of them, and below him, a certain amount of debris.

'They crumbled,' said Miss Skinner, 'when I stood on them.'

'What's it like down there?' asked Owen.

'Like—?'

'The ground. Is it OK to stand on?'

'Apart from the mummies, yes. It's like this.'

Owen gave Paul his torch and swung himself down. As his feet touched the ground he felt something give way and a cloud of acrid dust rose up and made him cough.

'Of course,' said Miss Skinner above him, 'when I fell, I landed on top of them. I suppose, in fact, they cushioned my fall. But the dust! I couldn't breathe! I thought I would choke.'

Owen reached his hand up for the torch. The chamber was long, about thirty feet, and, as far as he could see, filled with mummies.

'Why go to these lengths,' asked Paul, 'for animals?'

'They were sacred. I think, however,' said Miss Skinner, 'they must have had a fondness for them, too.'

The walls of the chamber were of granite blocks, exactly as the walls of the other room had been, fitting so well together that there wasn't even a slight toe-hold that Miss Skinner could have used.

The ground was deep in debris.

'I used a lot of mummies,' said Miss Skinner.

Owen gave Paul the torch and heaved himself up.

'Satisfied?' asked Miss Skinner. 'Have I told the truth?'

'I'm just trying to get a picture.'

Back in the corridor, he shone the torch around him.

'I still don't see how you came to fall.'

'I think I may have tripped,' said Miss Skinner, 'put my hand out, as one does, found nothing there, overbalanced and fallen through.'

Owen dropped on one knee and began to run his hands over the floor.

'But what could you have tripped on?'

'Is there nothing there? I thought I caught an edge. Of course, in the dark—'

Owen straightened up and began to feel round the walls.

'Perhaps it was my own flat feet,' said Miss Skinner. She gave a little laugh. 'I seem to be making rather a habit of it, don't I?'

'What didn't you like about it?' asked Owen.

'It was what she said when we got her out,' said Paul. 'She said she'd been pushed.'

'She said it as definitely as that?'

'Yes. It was as we were helping her back along the passage. I said to her, you know, the way one does: "My God, Miss Skinner, what's happened to you?" And she said: "I was pushed and fell into that dreadful place." Something like that. But definitely pushed.'

'She's not saying that now.'

'No, and a bit later, when we'd cleaned her up, and given her a drink, and she'd rested and I asked her again—I wanted to get the detail—she wasn't saying it then, either. She just said she must have fallen. And when I probed, she shut up like a clam.'

'Wouldn't say any more?'

'Stuck to a "Silly me—a foolish accident" kind of routine. But that's not what she said when we got her out.'

'Changed her mind when she'd had time to think about it.'

'Yes. I must say,' said Paul, 'that I find the "Silly me" routine more than a little implausible in the case of Miss Skinner. A more self-possessed lady I have seldom encountered.'

'Yes. Piling up the mummies—or even feeling them in the dark to find out what kind of mummies they were—does not seem to me the act of someone who's lost her head.'

'She was shaken, all right,' said Paul. 'She'd had a fall and she'd been down there all right. But confused? I wouldn't have said she was at all confused.'

'So you thought it was all a bit fishy?'

'There were other things, too. I went back down the passage and had a look and I couldn't see how she could have come to have fallen. And then,' said Paul, 'I remembered how she'd been pushed, and I decided that I was asking myself too many questions, and that they were not aide-de-camp sort of questions but Mamur Zapt sort of questions.'

Last of all, Parker took them to a small chapel, only about ten feet long and five feet wide. The walls were covered with sculptures carved in relief and painted, and the roof was painted too, blue with yellow stars.

'It is, of course, the sky,' said Miss Skinner. 'I like that, don't you? The cow grazing in the field, with the blue sky above.'

For this was the famous chapel in which Naville had discovered the Cow of Hathor.

'What a piece of luck!' said Parker enviously.

'Not luck,' corrected Miss Skinner. 'Sound archæological practice. He'd worked out the chapel was going to be there.'

'He didn't know there was going to be anything like the Cow of Hathor in it, though, did he?'

Parker turned to Owen.

'The trouble with these places,' he said, 'is that even when you get into a chamber, you don't know there's going to be anything there. And that's for two reasons: first, because if there was anything there, it's probably been stolen; second, because the people who put it there in the first place anticipated that it might be stolen and hid it somewhere else. You need luck as well as archæology. And shall I tell you something else?'

He faced Miss Skinner belligerently.

'You also need to be a bit of a thief yourself, to figure out how their minds worked!' He laughed loudly.

'And are you?' asked Miss Skinner.

He broke off and looked at her, amused.

'I'm just a simple archæologist,' he said. 'That's why I'm not likely to find anything!'

He ushered them out. They stood for a moment blinking in the bright sunlight. Parker looked around.

'You ask yourself if there could be another one nearby. If that one was intact, maybe they didn't touch this part of the site. There might be another one. Still,' he said, 'that's a question I'm not allowed to ask myself.'

'Why not?'

He shrugged.

'It's the licence,' he said. 'I'm only allowed to work in two places: the sanctuary and the North-East Court.'

He led them back into the shade of the colonnade and then turned to Owen.

'Well,' he said, 'that it? Seen all you want? Can I go now, sir? Some of us have work to do.'

'If Mr el Zaki has finished with you,' said Owen coldly. He did not like the way Parker addressed all his remarks to him.

'For the moment,' said Mahmoud.

Parker walked off without giving him a look. After a little hesitation, Miss Skinner followed him, saying that she was going to see how work in the sanctuary was progressing. Paul, taking no chances now, went with her.

Work was also going on in the North-East Court. There was a colonnade on one side and under it some workmen were prising the façade off an inner wall. The façade, carved and painted like the walls of the chapel they had just seen, sagged forward and was held up by props.

Sand from the desert had drifted into the open colonnade over the centuries and raised its floor level by three or four feet. To free the base of the façade, the men had had to dig down. There were two of them in the trench now, clearing away the last bit of hard sand from the pediment.

Mahmoud said something to them and one of the workmen looked up, wiped the sweat from his face with his forearm and climbed out.

He took hold of two of the props supporting the façade and shook them vigorously. They did not budge. The workman nodded his head to Mahmoud as if to say 'There you are!' smiled and climbed back.

'All the same,' Mahmoud said to Owen, 'that's what happened.'

He took Owen further along the colonnade to a part where the façade had already been stripped off.

'It happened here. They got four-fifths of the way through and then the next morning, early, two men went back to finish the job. One of them was in the trench when the prop gave way.'

'Anyone check the props?'

'The foreman should. But these men are experts. They come from the local village, Der el Bahari, and are used to working on archæological sites. They say they've been doing the kind of thing since they were born and don't need a foreman.'

'What about the one who was killed? Hadn't he been doing it ever since he was born, too?'

'As a matter of fact, he hadn't. They said he wasn't one of them. He came from a different village.'

'What does Parker say?'

'The men are right. They know what they're doing and don't make mistakes of this sort. The two workmen must have done something themselves. Disturbed the props, perhaps.'

'What about the other workman, the one who wasn't killed? Was he from another village, too?'

'No. I've talked to him. He swears he didn't touch the props. But the other man might have. While he himself was going off to fetch the tools. He says he hadn't worked with the other man much and didn't know him very well. He had the name of being a careless workman.'

Owen looked out from the colonnade, across the court-yard gashed with trenches and heaped with little piles of rubble, and out across the plain with its heat spirals coming and going.

'Half the accidents in this country are caused by careless-ness,' he said.

'Yes,' said Mahmoud, 'but is it the carelessness of the workers or of those who employ them?'

CHAPTER 5

When Owen went back later in the day the façade had been completely detached. It was lying in a corner of the courtyard with a number of other objects: the decapitated torso of a colossus, broken capitals exquisitely sculpted with designs of lotus stems and buds, fragments of wall fitted together jigsaw-like to yield a vivid mural of a field in harvest time, reapers bent to the sheaves.

The façade itself, however, was perhaps most striking of all. It was part of extended sculpting which ran the whole length of the colonnade. Cut in bas-relief, never more than a third of an inch deep, were delicate representations of ships with all their intricate cordage, their crews and merchandise, and in the waters below all the fishes of the Nile and the Red Sea.

There, too, was the port, and beyond that the villages of the interior with their thatched huts and people going about their daily business, all carved with intimate knowledge and consummate skill.

'Come to see the loot?' asked a crisp voice beside him.

It was Miss Skinner, armed with parasol and lorgnette, which she poked in the general direction of the exhibits.

'Would you like a guided tour?'

She tucked an arm beneath his and led him along the fragments of façade.

'This depicts an exhibition to the Land of Punt. Here are the spices—that's what they went for—and here is a leopard, a cub, I trust, being brought on board.'

A man dressed in European clothes came into the courtyard, followed by two workmen in galabeahs. He was, however, not a European but an Egyptian, from his face a Copt.

He glanced at a sheet of paper he was holding in his hand

and then tapped one of the capitals with his foot. The two workmen bent, lifted it on to their shoulders and staggered off.

'Is that a list? May I see it, please?' said Miss Skinner, holding out her hand.

The man hesitated.

'I'm sure Mr Parker would be glad to let you have a copy,' he said.

'That won't be necessary. It is merely a matter of an item or two which I would like to check.'

The man was still reluctant.

Miss Skinner took the paper from him.

'Thank you,' she said.

She perused the list for a moment.

'The sarcophagus,' she said: 'where is that?'

'Gone already.'

'And were there not some smaller pieces?'

'They were in the first load.'

'They are not on the list.'

'This is just the second page of the list.'

'Have you got the first page?'

'It went with the consignment.'

'What list is this?' asked Owen.

'All finds have to be listed,' said Miss Skinner. 'The list is then sent to the Museum.'

'I was sending the things anyway,' said the man, 'so I sent the list with them. It makes it easier for the Museum.'

'You work for the Museum?'

'No,' said the man. 'I work for Mr Parker.'

'This is Tomas,' said Miss Skinner, with a vague introductory wave of her hand, continuing to examine the list.

'I look after the transport,' said the Copt.

'It all goes up to the Museum? All this stuff?'

'Yes.'

'It's *all* going to be exported?'

'No, no. There are two different things. These are only going up for inspection.'

'All finds have to be recorded,' said Miss Skinner. 'Then, if they're movable, they have to be sent up to the Museum. That's a requirement of the licence. A means of control.'

'I see. And after that, they're the property of the Museum?'

'Would they were,' said Miss Skinner. 'Would they were.'

'What happens to them, then?'

'If it's an excavation conducted by the Department of Antiquities, the items pass into the custody of the Museum. If it's a private excavation, a disposition has to be agreed. In practice, if it's financed from abroad, most of the finds go abroad.'

'So they are exported, then?'

'The Museum keeps some.'

'And some are returned to the Pasha,' said the Copt softly.

'The Pasha?'

'The Pasha Marbrouk.'

'Why him?'

The Copt looked surprised.

'It is his land,' he said, almost reprovingly.

'The site, or part of it, is on the Pasha's estates,' said Miss Skinner.

'I see. So he has a claim to whatever is found?'

'He thinks,' said Miss Skinner.

It was getting dark and work had finished for the day. A last flash of sun was turning the tops of the cliffs coppery but, just below, the shadow was creeping rapidly towards them and down on the plain it was already dark.

Some workmen had lit a fire and were gathered round it drinking tea. One of them was singing softly.

Miss Skinner came out of her tent and sauntered off in the direction of the main temple. Paul, reading a book a little way away by the light of an oil lamp, snapped it shut and went after her.

'Really, Mr Trevelyan,' said Miss Skinner, 'you needn't.'

'It's a pleasure, Miss Skinner,' replied Paul blandly. 'I hope to benefit again from your erudition.'

'If that's all it is,' said Miss Skinner tartly, 'the lessons can stop right now.'

She swung on her heel and walked away. Her irritation was obvious.

Paul, not apparently in the least put out, followed after her. Owen had the feeling that Paul had expected him to play the role of bodyguard. He wanted, however, to talk to Mahmoud.

The Egyptian was standing by himself at the edge of the camp. He had spent most of the day talking to Parker, who was now, though, nowhere to be seen. Owen had the feeling, again, that Mahmoud was being deliberately made to feel unwelcome.

He went across and stood beside him.

'How's it going?'

'Not well.'

'What's the problem!'

'The men won't talk.'

Around the fire, by themselves, the men seemed voluble enough. They were chattering contentedly. Someone started a song and there was a burst of laughter.

'Frightened?'

Mahmoud indicated the group.

'Doesn't sound it,' he said.

'Too well paid.'

'It goes together,' said Mahmoud. 'They've got a good job and they don't want to lose it. All the same . . .'

Somebody lit a lamp over by the temple. Owen thought for a moment it might be Paul but then saw there was another little group of workmen camped beneath the wall. In the light he suddenly caught the face of Tomas.

Back at the fire the song had succeeded in getting itself established. It was a question-and-answer song, probably ribald. A young boy sang the questions, the others joined in the answers. There was considerable merriment.

'That,' said Mahmoud, 'is what I find puzzling.'

'The singing? It's traditional, this far south—'

'I've been on sites,' said Mahmoud, 'where workmen have been killed. There's an atmosphere. It just isn't there.'

'Maybe they've just accepted it. An accident, you know. These things happen.'

'Two accidents? In a short space of time? They don't accept that. Not at any site that I've been on.'

'If they genuinely thought it was an accident—'

'They blame the boss,' said Mahmoud with conviction. 'They always blame the boss.'

Owen shrugged.

'Maybe it's the money this time.'

He could see the problem from Mahmoud's point of view, but thought perhaps he was making too much of it. He knew what Mahmoud wanted; he wanted a conviction. But maybe it genuinely was something that could not be helped and the men knew it and that's why they weren't resentful. And maybe they'd told Mahmoud everything and it was just that he couldn't accept it.

'One accident I could believe in,' said Mahmoud, almost echoing Owen's thoughts. 'But two!'

'There are always a lot of accidents in any digging work,' Owen said.

Mahmoud was silent. Then he turned his face to Owen.

'Kismet? Is that it?' He laughed, a short, sharp bark of a laugh. 'You're the fatalist,' he said, 'not me.'

Mahmoud was definitely not a fatalist. It was that, perhaps, which made him a Nationalist. Like many young educated Egyptians, he looked around him and saw a country sunk in torpor. Idealistic, he wanted to do something about it. Blaming the system, he wanted to change it; and that led him, as it did so many others in the Law, the Police, the Army, towards the Nationalist Party.

The Nationalist Party was something new in Egyptian politics. But then, political parties were themselves something new in Egypt. The Khedive was a hereditary ruler and he chose his Ministers, his Government, from among his hereditary allies: the great Pashas, the equivalent of the landed aristocracy in England. And just as in England the rule of the Aristocrats had come to an end, so now in Egypt the rule of the Pashas was being challenged.

Mahmoud believed, Owen knew, that they should be swept away and replaced by a parliamentary democracy. But in Egypt there was an added complication; it wasn't the Pashas now who actually ran the country, but the British. Mahmoud believed they should be swept away, too.

Meanwhile, however, Owen and Mahmoud got on very amicably.

Owen thought, though, that Mahmoud's Nationalist sympathies might very well be tingeing his approach to this investigation. Parker was, in Mahmoud's view, a foreign exploiter and one, moreover, whose carelessness had resulted in the deaths of two unfortunate Egyptians working under him.

He shrugged. It wasn't really his concern.

What was his concern, he asked himself? Looking after that batty woman, he supposed, and seeing she didn't come to harm. This evening, though, in the blessed coolness of the dusk and with the men singing peacefully round the fire, there seemed little prospect of that.

Perhaps Owen was being unnecessarily alarmist.

The singing came to an end and the men at the first fire stood up. They seemed to have picks and spades with them, which they shouldered preparatory to setting off.

One of them was about to scatter the embers when another man put out his hand to restrain him, motioning towards the other group of workmen huddled against the wall. The first man laughed and then scattered the ashes deliberately and thoroughly.

The group set off.

As they passed the group beside the wall one of the recumbent men lifted his head and said something.

The men stopped and turned. Both groups fell silent.

Then one of the men took his spade off his shoulder and said something. Someone replied, and then the group at the wall was standing up and the other group unshipping their spades and picks.

Mahmoud was suddenly no longer beside Owen.

A man stepped into the space between the two groups and seemed to be pleading with them, or ordering them. He was definitely ordering the group at the wall. Then he turned to the others and seemed to be arguing with them. As he turned, his face caught the light and Owen saw that it was Tomas.

His intervention didn't seem to be working. The group with the spades edged forward. A man stepped out from the group at the wall, said something hotly and raised a stick.

Tomas started to make one last effort, then looked up and saw Mahmoud advancing towards them. He said something to the men. They looked up and hesitated.

'Want some help?' said Owen. His shoes crunched heavily on the sand.

'I don't think so,' said Mahmoud, stepping between the groups.

Tomas pushed the man with the stick back into the group by the wall. The others, with some show of reluctance, shouldered their spades. Two of the older ones started urging them away.

'Get off!' said Owen, coming up behind them.

He and Mahmoud stood there until the group was well on its way. Tomas came up to them, mopping his brow despite the coolness of the evening.

'Stupid!' he said. 'Stupid!'

'What's it all about?' asked Mahmoud.

Tomas shrugged. 'They are from the village,' he said. 'That is all.'

'And these are not?' He indicated the group by the wall.

'They came with me,' said Tomas.

'They're your workmen?'

'Yes.' Tomas wiped his brow again. 'Don't worry,' he said. 'In a day to two we'll be gone.'

Two of his men walked over to the scattered remnants of the fire and kicked them together again. Someone produced a kettle and stuck it on. Gradually the whole group wandered across. Except for one man who went on sitting angrily against the wall.

The moonlight now was making the sand silvery. Up above the line of the cliffs the sky was clear, almost frosty. It felt strange to Owen, used to the city, to see the stars in such profusion. The moon lit up the white front of the temple making it almost as light as day on the terraces.

Miss Skinner and Paul had still not returned.

Owen went over to the fire with its ring of squatting workmen. Tomas's face looked up at him.

'Can I borrow a couple of your men? I think I'm going to have to go looking for Miss Skinner and Trevelyan Effendi and I don't know the temple.'

'They don't know it, either,' said Tomas, getting to his feet. 'They're just porters. They carry the loads to the river. They've not been inside.'

'It would be handy to have someone with a torch.'

Tomas spoke to the men. Usually if you asked Egyptian workmen to help in a thing like this they responded with alacrity. These men didn't.

Tomas sharped his words and two of the men got up suddenly.

'They don't like going into the temple,' said Tomas apologetically. 'Not after what happened.'

'What happened?'

'The accidents.'

Light suddenly dawned.

'The man who was killed—he was one of your men? Not one of the diggers?'

'Both men,' said Tomas shortly, and turned away. 'I'll get torches,' he said over his shoulder. 'I'll see you on the lower terrace.'

The two workmen followed him unenthusiastically.

Over by the wall Owen saw Mahmoud talking to one of the workmen, the angry one, still evidently refusing to join his fellows around the fire.

Owen walked up the ramp leading to the lower terrace. At the top he hesitated. He had no idea which way to go. Miss Skinner and Paul might have gone anywhere.

Tomas joined him, holding a torch. The two workmen were also carrying torches, the big, kerosene-soaked ones used inside the temple. Out here in the moonlight they were redundant, mere pinpricks of light.

Tomas stepped into the colonnade and raised his torch. By its light Owen saw a forest of receding pillars with dark spaces between and behind them. There was no obvious path through them.

Owen walked past Tomas, deep into the forest, to where it was all dark. He looked carefully into the darkness for any answering pinprick, shifting his position in case it was masked by pillars. He saw nothing, however.

He waited a little while and then came out.

'Let's go up to the next terrace,' he said.

The workmen, relieved that he was not going further in, came more willingly this time.

He repeated the process on the second terrace and then again on the third. On the top terrace Tomas went in with him and gave a great shout. As the echoes died away they listened carefully but there was no answering call.

They descended to the lower terraces and shouted there too, but still there was no reply.

When they came out, Tomas looked at him.

Owen stood uncertainly. There was no point in plunging at random into the depths of the temple. It would be better to wait for daylight and the return of the diggers. There was, after all, still no real reason to suppose that anything had happened to Paul and Miss Skinner. A small voice, though, was beginning to whisper: surely not *again?*

He set off down the ramp. The stone of the courtyard below was white in the moonlight, except that close in to the wall of the ramp there was a little patch of shadow. When he got to the bottom he turned back into the court and went back to it.

It was the door which led down to the sanctuary and also to the chamber into which Miss Skinner had fallen previously. He told Tomas to wait outside with the torches and then walked down into the tunnel, guiding himself with his hand against the wall.

When he was well away from the light of the torches he stopped and looked. There was no light, just the rough touch of the wall and continuing, deepening, musty darkness.

He tried to remember whether there was a turn in the tunnel and decided there was, the room where one fork had led on down to the sanctuary and another had gone off down to what he thought of as Miss Skinner's chamber.

He went back out to where the men were waiting and told them to follow him. They did so unwillingly.

This time the descent seemed endless. It was partly that the men crept along, examining every bit of ground, their torches held high, before they moved. Well, that was not stupid, given what had happened to Miss Skinner, or what she said had happened to her. But he missed the casual assurance of the Der el Bahari diggers.

They came to the tunnel leading off to where she had fallen. Owen decided it would be foolhardy to go down that without more knowledgeable people. There might be other spots where the wall was weak or the floor crumbling. No, he would go down to the sanctuary, look there and then come back.

As they went on down the shaft, the men became more and more reluctant. Owen was afraid they might bolt back up the tunnel, so shepherded them ahead of him.

As he turned to chivvy one of them on he glanced back up the tunnel behind him. A few yards beyond the light cast by his own torches the darkness closed in again.

Except that there was—surely?—a faint touch of light.

He walked back towards it. It was coming from the gallery which led off to the right, towards Miss Skinner's chamber. It must be them! He quickened his pace.

And then the light went out!

He stopped, bewildered and unable to see. Everything was as pitch-black as, well, yes, the grave. He put his hand out to the wall to reassure himself.

Still there was no light. What had happened?

And then he became aware that someone was moving. He could hear steps in what must be the other gallery. They were careful, deliberate steps and were approaching the place where the gallery joined the main tunnel. But why no light?

Someone stepped out into the tunnel. There was a surprised exclamation. Owen realized suddenly that although he couldn't see, he himself could be seen by the light of the torches behind him.

'Christ, Owen!' said a startled voice. 'What are you doing here?'

It was Parker.

'I might ask you that!'

'Checking the workings. We don't want any more accidents, do we?'

'What, at night?'

'What are you doing here, anyway?' asked Parker, disregarding him.

'Trying to find Skinner and Trevelyan.'

'That damned woman?' Parker's anger was genuine. 'Always prowling around. Why doesn't Trevelyan keep her away?'

'Perhaps he has. I don't know that they are down here. It was just that I thought there might be a chance. They went out and they're not back yet. I was beginning to think—'

'That bloody woman? What business has she got to be prowling around? This is a private site, you know.'

'You can tell her. Why did you put out the light?'

'I thought I saw a light, your light, and I wanted to be sure. As a matter of fact, you may be right. I thought there was someone in here. That's why I came down.'

There was a shout from Owen's workmen. Owen ran down the tunnel towards them. They screened their torches with their bodies and pointed down the tunnel. A light was coming towards them.

'Hallo-o!' called a voice.

It was Paul's.

'Why!' said Miss Skinner. 'The tunnel is becoming quite populated!'

'What the bloody hell are you doing here?' said Parker, losing his temper.

'Well, what the bloody hell *were* you doing there?' asked Owen.

'She wanted to go there,' said Paul. 'She said she wanted to look at the sanctuary,'

'And did she?'

'Oh yes. She went over it with a fine-tooth comb. And

explained it all to me. In detail. In very considerable detail.
I think,' said Paul, 'that she was paying me back.'

'Paying you back?'

'I don't think she was altogether grateful for my
company.'

'You'd have thought she'd have learned,' said Owen.

'Yes. It's curious.'

Owen reflected.

'Was she looking for something, do you think? Something
particular?'

'That's what I wondered.'

Paul hesitated.

'If she was,' he said, 'I don't think she was looking for it
down in the sanctuary.'

'Then where—?'

'As we were going down,' said Paul, 'we came to that
other gallery—you know, the one going off to the left.
Where she'd been the night she fell. She seemed to hesitate
and said: "I suppose if I said I wanted to go down there
again, you'd tell me I was foolish?" "I certainly would," I
said. She laughed and said: "Sensible Mr Trevelyan! Let
us go on, then, to the sanctuary." But I got the feeling that
after that she was just, well, playing a game. Paying me
back.'

'Why don't we go down the other gallery?' said Owen.

As they went into the courtyard they met Mahmoud and
Parker. Parker was looking triumphant, Mahmoud
impassive.

'Where are you going?' asked Parker.

'I wanted to take another look at that gallery,' said
Owen, 'the one Miss Skinner was in when she fell.'

'It's nothing to do with the gallery,' said Parker. 'It's just
that damned stupid woman not taking precautions.'

'Like the workmen?' said Mahmoud.

Parker gave him a measured look.

'Yes,' he said, 'like the workmen. They shouldn't have been there. They're not diggers.'

'Then why were they digging?' asked Owen.

He wasn't going to let Parker ride roughshod over Mahmoud.

'Only one of them was,' said Mahmoud softly.

'And he oughtn't to have been,' said Parker. 'Thought he could earn a few extra piastres, I suppose.'

'Someone must have agreed to it.'

'It was that fool J'affar. I've spoken to him.'

He looked at Mahmoud. 'There have been mistakes,' he said. 'I'll acknowledge that. But not negligence. Not on my part. And no cutting corners on the safety. You ask the men. The real men, I mean, the ones who are actually doing the digging.'

Again there was the look of barely concealed triumph.

Mahmoud said nothing.

'We'll need torches,' said Owen.

Parker nodded.

'OK,' he said, and shouted to a passing workman. 'I'll come with you.'

When they came to the place where Miss Skinner had fallen, Parker lifted his torch and shone it through the hole.

'Want to have a look? It's just the same as it was. Mummies, mummies, mummies.'

'They're of no interest? Archæologically?'

'Not really. Not unless they're different. There are thousands of them in Egypt. Not even worth listing.'

He brought the torch back.

'All right? Seen enough?'

'Let's go on to the end of the gallery,' said Owen.

Parker shrugged. 'OK. If you want.'

The gallery ended after another fifty yards or so in a small, square room which was completely bare.

'This is all there is?'

'This is all there is. Disappointing.'

'It's a long way to cut a special tunnel. What's the point of it?'

'Well,' said Parker, 'you never know. One of the things they used to do was build extra chambers, concealed ones, in which they used to put the really valuable things. If there was something really valuable in that sanctuary, for instance, some relic, like the Cow, say, they might not have actually left it in the sanctuary but put it somewhere near. They got wised up, you see. They knew if they left something, people would be back.'

'The ones who built it?'

'Probably. From the village, anyway. Continuous tradition of robbery for three thousand years,' said Parker admiringly. 'And the buggers are still at it!'

He shone the torch around.

'Seen all you want to see?'

As they came out into the bright sunlight of the court, Owen said: 'Do you think Miss Skinner knows about the concealed chambers bit?'

Parker stopped. His face tightened.

'She was snooping,' he said, 'if that's what you mean.'

'What was she looking *for*?'

'How would I know?' said Parker, and walked away.

CHAPTER 6

'Like a picture,' said Paul, looking back at the great sweep of cliff with the temple nestling at its foot and the incredible clear blue sky above.

The rock had the lustre of burnished gold or copper— neither red nor brown, but a subtle blend of both, varying continuously as the sunlight moved over it. The temple was like mellowed ivory, yellow with age where the sun had fallen on it over the centuries, still dazzlingly white in places of shade.

'At least,' said Paul, 'they can't sell that.'

Owen looked at him.

'Is that how you feel?'

'A bit.'

They carried on across the sand to the second, lesser temple, where the day's work was already in progress. They could see figures working in the courtyard and a huge-wheeled wooden cart drawn up outside.

'I used to know a bit about archæology,' said Paul. 'I read Greats.'

'Greats?'

'Classics. That's what they call Latin and Greek at Oxford.'

Owen had studied Latin himself at a small Welsh grammar school and had at one time even entertained hopes of going to university; but then his father had died and there had been no money and instead he had gone straight from school into the army. On the whole he did not regret it, but sometimes he vaguely felt that he had missed something.

There was another thing, too, which he had become more conscious of when he moved from India to Egypt and joined the civil administration. The senior civil posts were all filled by people who had been to Oxford or Cambridge. It was like a club from which you had been excluded.

'Not the same, of course,' Paul was saying. 'Egyptology is a bit out on its own. But in our Ancient History course we used a lot of archæological evidence and I suppose I picked up something about scholarship, attitudes, that sort of thing. Well . . .'

'Yes?'

He shook his head.

'This isn't it.'

In the courtyard there was the flash of something white, a woman's dress.

'Old Peripoulin—' began Owen.

'He's all right: so are the people in Antiquities. It's, well . . .'

'Parker?'

'And people like him.'

'Miss Skinner spoke of his methodology.'

'I wouldn't know anything about that. It's just that he's, well, stripping the place, isn't he?'

'He's got a licence.'

'A licence to pillage,' said Paul. 'Something for you to look into, boyo, when you get back.'

The white figure was definitely Miss Skinner. She was talking to the workmen. Owen wondered how she was getting on. As far as he knew she spoke no Arabic.

Not very well, probably, for when Tomas came into the courtyard she at once attached herself to him.

'But where are they?' Owen heard her saying.

'They were on the second load,' said Tomas in his slow, courteous English.

'How many loads have there been?'

'This is the fourth.'

Miss Skinner looked around the courtyard suspiciously.

'There was a cartouche,' she said. 'Where is it?'

Tomas pointed to the cart on the other side of the wall.

Miss Skinner walked across and examined the contents. There was, indeed, even Owen could see, a cartouche among them. A cartouche was an oval cut in stone with a number of hieroglyphics inside it, usually the name of a royal personage. Cartouches were extremely common on walls of temples.

Miss Skinner came back.

'It's not on the list,' she said.

'It's on another list,' said Tomas patiently.

Miss Skinner pounced.

'I thought you told me the other day that the list went with the load?'

'So it does. The goods arrive at the Museum as a single load and the list is presented with them. They are, however, despatched separately and the individual sheets of the list do not always coincide exactly with the consignments.'

'The goods are despatched as separate loads?'

'Yes.'

'Why is that?'

'It is cheaper,' said Tomas, still patiently though with a certain weariness. 'They go on a boat when there is space.'

'Where are they brought together?'

'At Heraq.'

'Heraq?'

'It is a port this side of Cairo. I prefer to use it because it is a small port. Bulak—the main port of Cairo—is too big and things can easily go astray.'

'And up to that point,' said Miss Skinner, 'the separate sheets of the list do not correspond to particular consignments?'

'That is correct.'

Miss Skinner sniffed.

'I find it very unsatisfactory. How do you know, when something is missing, which load it belonged to?'

'I keep my own records,' said Tomas faintly.

'Ah! Can I see them?'

Tomas gave her some handwritten sheets.

'But these are in Arabic!' said Miss Skinner, disappointed.

'Yes,' said Tomas.

Miss Skinner was for the moment nonplussed. Tomas turned back to his workmen. They began to carry another piece out to the cart.

Miss Skinner looked up and saw Owen and Paul. She seemed disconcerted, but then advanced boldly upon them.

'I have been checking on the transport arrangements,' she announced. 'I find them less than satisfactory.'

'Oh?'

'The recording leaves much to be desired.'

'Really?'

'It would be very easy for something to go missing.'

'Would it not be even easier,' said Owen, 'if the thing were not recorded at all?'

Miss Skinner looked at him sharply.

'Everything has to be recorded,' she said. 'That is the first principle of archæology.'

'And of the licensing system, too. But suppose it isn't?'

Again Miss Skinner seemed disconcerted.

'But that would be dishonest,' she said. 'Surely one has to trust the integrity of the archæologist. Doesn't one?'

It was noon and sizzlingly hot. To touch the metal of one of the spades left lying in the courtyard was to give yourself something very like a burn. Even the woodwork was unpleasantly warm.

The men in the courtyard had abandoned loading the cart and retreated into the shade. Tomas was nowhere to be seen.

The Der el Bahari men were deep inside the temple where it was cool. A smell of burned beans came wafting out. Most workmen made a midday meal of just bread, but the Der el Bahari men had their own standards.

So, up to a point, had the cook, and Miss Skinner had made a pleasant lunch of tomato salad. She was sitting now in a canvas chair borrowed from Parker, reading a book.

Paul, too, was reading a book, reclining comfortably nearby on the sand.

'Really, Mr Trevelyan,' said Miss Skinner irritably, 'I am hardly likely to come to harm during my siesta!'

'I certainly hope that is the case,' said Paul, unperturbed. 'I was banking on an uninterrupted read.'

After a moment or two's reflection, Miss Skinner was not quite sure how to take this and returned to her pages.

Owen went in search of Mahmoud and found him talking

to one of the workmen, the rebellious one from Tomas's team. Owen would have gone away, not wishing to interrupt, but Mahmoud indicated with a welcoming jerk of his head that it was all right to join them.

'Because this is the Mamur Zapt,' he explained to the workmen.

The workman was a country peasant, and unimpressed. The Mamur Zapt was a by-word only in Cairo.

'He's only interested in the woman,' he said. 'And that's only because she's a Sitt and foreign.'

'He's interested in Abu and Rashid, too,' said Mahmoud softly.

'Is he? Well, it's time someone was. Abu was from my village,' he said to Owen. 'He was my sister's husband's cousin. Part of the family. So when they came round asking for men, I said I would go. Someone had to find out what had happened to him! Really happened to him.'

'What did you think had happened to him? Was it not an accident?'

The man made a gesture with his hand and spat into the sand. 'Accident!' he said. 'I'll tell you this: there isn't any such thing as an accident. There's always a reason.'

'And what do you think the reason was here?'

'I don't know,' the man growled. 'That's what I'm trying to find out. But I'll tell you this: I reckon he was on to something.'

'On to something?'

'Yes. Found out something he ought not to have found out. And so they killed him.'

'Killed!'

'That's right.'

'I thought you said it was an accident?'

'That's what *they* said. Accident!' He spat again.

'Which one was this?' Owen asked Mahmoud.

'The second one. He was found in a trench one morning with half a ton of earth on top of him.'

'They said he'd been wandering about at night. Fallen in. Brought the walls down on top of him. His fault, they said. Didn't look where he was going, and shouldn't have been there anyway. Drunk, more likely than not. Drunk!' said the man bitterly. 'Abu! A decent, God-fearing Moslem. Never touched a drop. Well, not often. Not here, anyway. Where would he have got it from? Hadn't been paid, had he? Nobody gets paid until the stuff is up at Heraq.'

'Drunk! said Mahmoud, commiserating. 'What a thing to say!'

'And the man so new in his grave, the angels have not even had time to examine him!'

'Outrageous!' said Mahmoud.

'A pack of lies, all of it!'

'Mind you,' said Mahmoud, 'you've got to ask what he was doing there at that time of night.'

'That's it! It's not as if there was a woman about.'

'You're sure there wasn't a woman about?'

'Over here? In the village, perhaps, not over here.'

'I wondered if one had come over.'

'Too far. In any case, those village women keep to themselves.'

'You see, that would explain it. Some husband, perhaps—'

'He'd have stuck a knife in him. Anyway, Abu wasn't that sort. Well, not often. And he'd hardly been here long enough.'

'True. That's true. And anyway he fell into a trench.'

'So they say.'

'You don't think so?'

'What I ask,' said the workman, 'is what he was wandering about for?'

'And what's your answer?'

'He was on to something. There was something going on and he wanted to find out what it was.'

'So he went out to look?'

'And found it. And they found him. And then—Bash!—that was it!'

'Terrible!' said Mahmoud, shaking his head commiseratingly.

'What do you think he found?' asked Owen.

The man looked over his shoulder and lowered his voice.

'Treasure,' he breathed. 'These Der el Bahari people know where it is, see? They've been robbing these tombs for centuries. They've got it all hidden away, somewhere. Let it out a bit at a time. Don't spoil the market, see? Oh, they're clever ones, everyone knows that. Well, it's my belief that Abu got on to it somehow. Had an idea where they kept it. Went to have a look and they caught him. Well, that was it, wasn't it? They had to finish him off. No choice, really. Didn't want him telling anyone else. A quick tap and there you are.'

'What about the trench?'

'Stuffed him in it and knocked the walls down. Made it look like an accident.'

There was a general shaking of head over man's criminality and ingenuity and then a little silence.

'And there it would have rested,' said Owen, as if philosophizing, 'if it hadn't been for the other man. One accident, well, things like that happen, don't they? But two! It makes you wonder.'

'You don't wonder very much,' the man said bitterly, 'if it's a peasant that's dead.'

'It makes me wonder,' said Mahmoud quietly.

'Well, perhaps you're different. Only it always seems to us that the city is a long way away and so is the Khedive, and no one cares very much about what happens up here and the Pasha's whip is still long.'

'Still?'

That, at any rate, had been one of the British achievements: the curbash, whipping, had been abolished.

'Still. As I said, the city's a long way away.'

'Even so,' said Mahmoud. 'I am here.'

The man gave an acknowledging nod of the head.

'You may be all right,' he said, 'and so may be your friend, for all I know, even though he's a foreigner. But you won't get anywhere. The Pasha's too big for you. He's too big for us. We're just little flies on his big wheel and when the wheel goes round we're the ones who get squashed.'

'Little stones,' said Mahmoud, 'can make big wheels jump.'

'Which are you,' asked the man, 'the stone or the wheel?'

'I'm one of those who are trying to change the wheel.'

'Yes,' said the man, 'so you said. There are people, you said, in the city who are trying to change things. The Nationalists, was it? Well, there aren't many Nationalists down here, I can tell you. And the city is still a long way away.'

About a mile beyond the temple, where the great spur of rock which separated the plain from the Sahara curved sharply round, was the village. It merged so completely into the cliffs that, looking across in the daytime, Owen had hardly been aware it was there. At night, however, when the villagers were cooking the evening meal, the lower slopes were covered with the pinpricks of their fires.

Approaching the village now, on mule-back, in the gathering dusk, Owen saw that the village was bigger than he had supposed. Children were playing among the boulders, women were busy in the courtyards at their buffalo-dung fires and men were sitting up on the roofs of their houses enjoying the evening breeze.

The houses were not the usual ones of the river bank, tidy cubes of mud brick, with the roofs heaped high with onions and water-melons and firewood. These were built among the rocks and the walls were often piled stones. They ran back in deep trenches into the cliff face, so that they seemed half underground.

There was no sociable communal square, no neat streets. The houses were scattered higgledy-piggledy over the slopes and the occupants sat on the roofs and shouted across to each other.

There were indeed onions and water-melons and not infrequently tomato plants and beans straggling up the sides of houses, but compared with the abundance of the river this was subsistence only.

Owen, used to the rich fields of the delta, was quite shocked. Yet in some curious way it seemed familiar. And then, seeing high up above the village the shafts of abandoned excavations, he realized suddenly what it was. This was a mining village.

'Grim!' said Paul, giving a little shudder of distaste.

'Hard!' said Owen, and realized suddenly that he was using the expression of the miners in the village he had known as a child.

The difference between the two expressions was the difference in perspective between the æsthete and the labourer. Owen had never been a labourer in that sense—his father had been an Anglican clergyman—but although on the periphery, he had known the shared life of a Welsh mining village. Now it came back to him unexpectedly. He felt suddenly that he knew the people here.

He did; although not quite in the way that he supposed.

As he slid off the back of his donkey, a surprised voice greeted him warmly.

'Effendi!' it said. 'You are my father and mother!'

'I doubt it,' said Owen, and then, seeing who had spoken, embraced the speaker warmly. 'Sayid!'

It was one of his favourite swindlers, last seen outside the Continental Hotel beguiling tourists with relics of dubious authenticity and patter of genuine imaginativeness. Astonished admiration of the patter had led Owen to pardon a few minor solecisms, thus laying the basis of a relationship which Sayid reasserted with eagerness every time he came to Cairo.

'You have come to visit my home,' said Sayid enthusiastically.

'That is not the sole purpose of my visit,' said Owen. 'Nevertheless, I rejoice at the opportunity.'

Sayid, chattering excitedly, led him up the cliff. As they gained in height, Owen, looking back, could see the roofs of the houses below him, the little walled courtyards, the winding, higgledy-piggledy paths which took the place of streets.

There, at a corner where a barber had set out his chair and bowl and a small group had gathered expectant of miracles, sat Mahmoud, deep in conversation; and there, on the other side of the village, assisted unexpectedly by Tomas, was Miss Skinner, talking earnestly to another knot of villagers.

'She gives baksheesh,' said Sayid approvingly, 'plenty baksheesh.'

'You know her?' said Owen, surprised.

'Oh yes.'

'And what does she give baksheesh *for*?'

Sayid looked injured.

'Not *for*, out of. Out of the liberality of her hand, out of the generosity of her heart, out of—'

'I know the lady, too,' Owen cut in. 'What is she giving baksheesh for? Things that you have found? Or is it things that you know?'

'I do not understand that latter point,' said Sayid. 'We have tried offering her things that we have found. Alas, she knows whether we have truly found them. She gives good prices for what is genuine. Unfortunately, we are running out of that sort of thing.'

'Business is bad, is it?'

'Terrible. It won't pick up until it get cooler again and the tourists come back.'

'Meanwhile, you're getting a few things together. I expect?'

'A few,' said Sayid non-committally.

Sayid's house was at the top of the village, a gash in the rock covered over with slabs of limestone and sparsely furnished inside. Owen got the impression the inside wasn't used very much. There was a bed-roll on the roof, which suggested that Sayid and his wife slept up there. Cooking was done on a brazier in the yard, and it was from there that Sayid's wife shortly brought them cups of tea.

She also brought two very small children. Owen complimented Sayid on a growing family. Sayid, however, seemed a little depressed.

'Both girls,' he said. 'If she goes on like this, I don't know what I shall do. Have to get another one, I suppose.'

'Child?'

'Wife.'

Owen shook his head, commiserating.

'The trouble is, it all costs money,' said Sayid gloomily.

They sat on the roof watching the dusk close down and the stars come out. The only lights in the village came from the braziers in the yards and the occasional tallow lamp where someone was still working. The smell of fried onions rose strongly through the evening air.

'Ya Sayid!'

It was somebody hailing from a neighbouring roof. Sayid rose to his feet.

'They are finished. Come and see!'

Sayid hesitated.

'Do not let me stand in your way,' said Owen politely. 'I must go now anyway.'

'You are sure?'

'I should go to see the woman. Perhaps she will offer me some baksheesh, too.'

Sayid laughed and they descended from the roof. As they

emerged on to what passed for the street, the neighbour came rushing over.

'Perfect!' he said. 'Perfect, this time. Come and see!'

He seized Sayid by the arm and then, encompassing Owen in his overspilling goodwill, caught him up too.

'I—' began Owen.

But the man was already urging them through a low doorway and into his house. Down by the river, in the houses that Owen knew, the first room was often given over to the family buffalo. This one was not. It was a workshop.

There were three windows, each giving light to a workman's bench strewn with scarabs, amulets and funerary statuettes in every stage of progress. Some were of wood, some limestone and some clay.

What the neighbour had brought them in to show them, however, were some five ushapti images of glazed faïence, newly made.

'Are they not good? My best work yet,' said the neighbour, standing proudly beside them.

Sayid looked uncomfortable.

'They are indeed fine—'

'Don't you like them?' cried the neighbour anxiously. 'Look! The glaze. My best yet!'

Sayid stole a glance at Owen.

'They are remarkable,' said Owen, picking up one of the figures. It was of a sower. The point of the images was that they were put in the tomb so that in the after-life they could work in the dead man's fields. 'As well made as any I have seen.'

'There you are!' said the neighbour, bursting with pride.

'Yes, but—' said Sayid unhappily.

'Look! This one!' said the neighbour, snatching up the figure of a ploughman bent to the plough. 'Is it not fine? The hands, you see? I always find it difficult to do the hands.'

'Exquisite.' Owen picked up another one. 'But what is this?' he said, puzzled.

The neighbour looked slightly abashed.

'It is one of us,' he said.

'A digger? But—?'

'He's in a trench, you see, over at the temple. He's bent, because he's digging. He's just going to shovel some out.'

'I see that. But—that is today, isn't it? And these others are of long ago.'

'Well, it's all work, isn't it? And I thought it would be nice to have some of us. This, actually, is Abdul.'

'Very nice. A nice idea. But—when it comes to selling it—?'

'Oh, they won't know. No, don't worry about that. They won't spot it. After all, one figure is very like another. Though I do think this one—'

Owen looked around him. Some of the images were coloured. There beside them were the colours and brushes. To say nothing of files, gravers and little pointed tools like gimlets. A magnifying-glass of the kind used by engravers lay on one of the benches. Screwed to the bench was a small grindstone worked by a treadle. And there, in a corner, was a huge fragment of mummy-case, which showed where the old sycamore for the wooden figures came from.

'You are well equipped,' said Owen.

'Have to be,' said the neighbour seriously. 'This is skilled work.'

'Indeed it is. But—isn't there good money to be had over at the temple?'

'It comes and goes. I mean, they're always digging some-where but sometimes it's a long way away and they don't always need many men. No, this is much better. You have to work hard, mind, but the money comes in regularly.'

'Even now?'

'Well, not so much now, of course, but when the men go out in a month or two's time they'll need all the stock they can get. These will fetch very good prices, won't they, Sayid?' he said, stroking his figures fondly.

'Er—yes,' said Sayid.

Owen sighed.

'A man's got to live,' said Sayid defensively.

'Ushapti images?' said Miss Skinner. 'No. I don't think so. Charming, but I have plenty.'

'Then what—?'

Miss Skinner gave him a sidelong glance.

'Well,' she said, 'these people have been plundering the tombs for centuries and in the process some fine things have come into their possession. It's always worth offering them a special price. You'd be surprised at the things they produce.'

'Not altogether,' said Owen.

CHAPTER 7

'*If*,' said Miss Skinner venomously, 'you could bear to deny me the pleasure of your company for even a few moments—'

'I have no wish to force myself upon you, Miss Skinner,' said Paul stiffly.

'Then don't,' said Miss Skinner and walked off.

A little later they saw her setting off across the desert in the direction of the village.

'What do I do? Go after her?' asked Paul.

'I wouldn't bother,' said Owen.

Paul grimaced.

'Sorry I brought you down,' he said. 'It all seems a bit of a waste of time.'

'It was reasonable. She said she'd been attacked.'

'And then she unsaid it. Afterwards. "Silly me." Only I don't think Miss Skinner is at all silly.'

'Nor do I. So why did she unsay it?'

'She obviously wanted to play it down.'

'And why would that be?'

'Because she didn't want too many questions being asked.'

'And then again, of course, one asks why that would be?'

'She was doing something that she ought not to be.' Paul frowned. 'Only that doesn't seem likely, does it? She seems to take it for granted that God is on her side.'

'And you're the chap who's hindering her from getting on with God's investigations.'

'So are you. She doesn't want you asking questions.'

'When we were in Cairo she was *glad* I was going to be asking questions.'

'Ah, but she's been in Egypt a bit longer now. Maybe she's abandoned hope. Of Egypt. Of you, old chap.'

'Thanks.'

'She thinks she can do better herself.'

'I don't blame her.'

'But if she thinks that,' said Paul, 'why cry for help? Because she *did* cry for help, you know when we pulled her out.'

'A wobble. A moment's self-doubt. Rare, for Miss Skinner. Probably unique. Knocked her off balance. Just for a moment.'

'And then she came on balance again and didn't want anything to do with us. Could handle it all herself.'

'But what,' said Owen, 'is *it?*'

'Ah, well there you have me. It all comes from being a stupid aide-de-camp and not the Mamur Zapt. You think she feels she's on to something?'

'On to something?' said Owen.

'Connected?' said Mahmoud. 'I wouldn't have thought so.'

'Your man yesterday said he thought Abu was on to something and that's why he was killed.'

'Everyone in Egypt thinks his neighbour is on to something. And then if he gets killed, that gets taken as proof.'

'He thought Abu might have been wandering around —'

'Looking for treasure. Yes, I know. That's another great myth. Everybody knows that the Der el Bahari villagers have been robbers for centuries, so it stands to reason that in that time they must have amassed a huge treasure. Of course, no one asks why if that's the case the present inhabitants spend their time selling relics for a living.'

'If everyone thinks so,' said Owen, 'Abu may have thought so.'

'And wandered round at night on the off-chance he'd find it?'

'Why else would he be wandering around?'

'Theft.'

'What of?'

'Equipment. Cable, that sort of thing. He was leaving in a day or two. Something small that he could smuggle.'

'So you don't think he was on to something?'

'No. Nor the other one. I'm treating them both as accidents. And I'm trying to find evidence of negligence.'

'Are you finding it?'

'No,' Mahmoud admitted. He looked up at the great rim of cliff. 'It's like that,' he said. 'A wall. A wall of silence. They won't say anything.'

'Your chap yesterday —''

'He had a grudge. He was prepared to talk. But he had nothing to say.'

'The others?'

'Tomas's men? Wouldn't say a word. A bit frightened, I think. The place, the people. Me. They're only here for a few days and then they'll be off. Keep your head down. Nothing to do with you.'

'Weren't the two who were killed Tomas's men?'

'Another crew. Didn't know them. They say.'

'And the villagers?'

'Nothing to do with them. Outsiders. Their own fault.'

'Can't you get anywhere on the negligence angle? Aren't they worried it might happen to them?'

'No.'

'Too well bribed?'

Mahmoud looked at him.

'If I could only prove that—!'

'And how long, Captain Owen, are you proposing to stay?' asked Miss Skinner sweetly, as they sat at supper.

'I think I may return tomorrow.'

'Indeed?'

Miss Skinner put down her fork.

'Then allow me to say, Captain Owen, how greatly I appreciate your solicitude. It was, perhaps, unnecessary, but that was my own fault, and I am truly grateful that you should go to such lengths. I shall convey that formally to the Government.'

Owen bowed acknowledgement.

'You and Mr Trevelyan.'

'Most kind of you, Miss Skinner,' said Paul, concentrating on his supper. 'I, of course, will not be returning with Captain Owen.'

'No?'

Miss Skinner picked up her fork.

'It's not necessary, you know.'

'I'm sure. However, I believe in keeping to arrangements.'

'A true aide-de-camp,' said Miss Skinner, attempting to spear a gherkin.

'I believe in keeping to arrangements, too,' said Parker. 'Only I like to know what they are. How much longer are you going to be here?' he said to Miss Skinner.

'I'm in no hurry,' said Miss Skinner, stabbing the gherkin successfully and raising it to her mouth.

'Oh, aren't you? Well, that's a pity. Because I am and you're getting in my way.'

'There's nothing to stop you getting on with what you're doing,' said Miss Skinner. 'I'm merely observing.'

'You're poking your nose in!' said Parker. 'That's what you're doing.'

Miss Skinner merely smiled.

'How long do I have to put up with this?' Parker demanded. He turned to Mahmoud. 'Come on, you're the expert. How long do I have to put up with it? Do I have to put up with it at all? It's not in the licence.'

'A lot of things are not in the licence,' said Mahmoud.

'Well, perhaps they should be. Perhaps there should be something about visitors. Because visitors take time and time costs money. The group I work for have put up a lot of money for this dig, their only money. We've got rights! We're bringing a lot of money into this country.'

'Any money you're bringing in, you're taking out,' said Mahmoud, and left the table.

'What are *you* doing?' said Parker, coming up behind Mahmoud.

Mahmoud was bent over examining the support stays in the colonnade. He did not reply.

'You won't find anything wrong,' said Parker. 'There or anywhere else. We know what we're doing.'

Mahmoud took out a notebook and wrote something down.

Parker gave the post a shake.

'It's firm,' he said. 'Firm as a rock. You'd better make sure that's what you're writing down.'

Mahmoud put the notebook away and went on to the next post. Parker watched him in baffled anger for a moment and then went across to Owen.

'Can't you get him off my back?' he said.

'Mr el Zaki's investigations are nothing to do with me.'

'Oh, aren't they? I thought the British ran everything in Egypt?'

'Not the law. We don't interfere with the judicial process.'

'Don't you? Well, it's the only bloody thing you don't interfere with. And if you don't, plenty of other people do. Money talks, doesn't it? And in Egypt it talks in a bloody shout. I've got the money, or at least the people who back me have, and I know what to do!'

'You're all right, then, aren't you?' said Owen and walked over to Mahmoud.

Mahmoud took hold of one of the supports and tried to shake it. It held firm. Mahmoud, however, took out his notebook and wrote something down.

Parker had followed Owen over.

'You won't be able to pin anything on me,' he said to Mahmoud. 'And do you know why? Because there isn't anything to pin.'

Mahmoud ignored him.

'But I'll tell you what,' said Parker, 'sure as hell, I'll pin something on you!'

Owen decided to take one last look at the place where Miss Skinner had been attacked, or might have been attacked. He asked Mahmoud to come with him and the Egyptian, who seemed to have finished his inquiries for the moment, readily agreed.

'There's not much more I can do here,' he said. 'In fact I might as well come back with you tomorrow. I can write the reports in Cairo as well as I can here.'

'You've got to that stage, have you?'

Mahmoud shrugged.

'Mainly because there's not much in the other stages. They won't talk. The post-mortem shows nothing out of the ordinary—frankly, the post-mortem practices up here leave much to be desired, but it's too late, really, to ship them to Cairo. The work practices, well, I've checked them, as you know, but work practices in Der el Bahari are a bit different from what they are elsewhere and, again, there is nothing really too much out of line.'

'No question of negligence, then?'

'There's the question of negligence, there's plenty of questions, but no real answer. And if the doubts are only at the question level, they won't bother to do anything.'

'He gets away with it?'

Mahmoud shrugged. 'He gets away with it.'

For Mahmoud, two principles came into opposition. On the one hand he was passionately committed to bringing wrongdoers to justice, believing that it didn't happen often enough in Egypt. On the other, a stickler for the law and proper process—because he felt there wasn't enough of that in Egypt either—he felt compelled to abide by requirements of proper proof.

Owen thought he was rather glad to get away for the moment from the inner wrestle.

They looked again at the corridor and again at the gap in the wall and then dropped down into the chamber into which Miss Skinner had fallen.

This time Owen had taken the precaution of equipping himself with a powerful lamp and so could see much better.

The chamber was about six feet high and ran back for some twenty or thirty feet. The roof was jet black, which at first he thought was paint but then, scraping it with a knife, found that it was a deposit formed, he guessed, by the exhalations from the bodies beneath.

The mummies ran back in rows to the other end of the chamber. They were piled five or six deep, except that in one place there was a large gap.

Mahmoud picked his way between the rows towards it and then stood looking at it for some time. Then he came back and heaved himself up out of the chamber and re-examined the gap in the wall.

Clearly puzzled, he dropped down again and this time went straight to the other end of the chamber.

Owen brought the light up to him. Mahmoud took it and shone it against the wall. There was what appeared to be a doorway but filled in. Mahmoud disregarded it.

'False door,' he said, and then went over the whole of the rear wall shining the lamp and feeling with his hands. Some mummies were in the way. He moved them and gave a grunt of satisfaction. He gave Owen the lamp and fell on his knees.

He was wrestling with what appeared to be part of the wall, but as he eased it forward Owen saw it to be a large separate stone. As it came out it revealed a gap behind.

Mahmoud took the lamp and shone it through. Then he pushed it through the gap and crawled after it. After a little hesitation Owen followed.

He found he was in another chamber similar to the first, although perhaps rather longer. It was full of mummies, piled high to the ceiling. Again there was that strange, sooty black.

There was a gap running up the middle of this chamber between the mummies, As he walked along it, his feet kept crunching on something and, looking down, he saw the floor was covered with broken bones and decayed mummy cloth.

Mahmoud touched some of the bones with his foot.

'Crocodiles,' he said.

The room was full of mummified crocodiles, hundreds of them, perhaps thousands. They lay in regular layers, head to tail and tail to head.

The bottom layer consisted of large crocodiles, side by side, each one carefully mummied and wrapped up in cloths. Smaller ones were laid between the tails, filling up the hollows; and then, crammed into all the interstices, were dozens upon dozens of young crocodiles.

Each one was about a foot long and stretched out between two slips of palm-leaf stem, bound to its sides like splints. It was then wrapped from foot to head in a strip of cloth, wound round, starting at the tail.

The layer was carefully covered with palm leaves and then another layer, exactly similar to the previous one, built on top of it. And so on till the chamber was piled high to the ceiling.

Except that again there was that curious gap.

This time Mahmoud inspected it curiously and then went straight to the rear wall.

'We could go on,' he said to Owen. 'Do you want to?'

'I don't understand.'

'There'll be another exit. Like the other one.'

'Who—?'

Mahmoud laughed.

'When?' he said. 'It will be the Der el Baharis, though whether this lot or their fathers or their great-great-grandfathers—'

'All right, then,' said Owen, 'but why? Isn't it just mummies? Or were they looking for treasure?'

'Treasure!' said Mahmoud dismissively. 'This is their treasure. Mummies. Haven't you seen those mummies they sell outside the Continental? Cats, hawks, crocodiles? This is where they come from. Or places like this.'

'They break in and—?'

'Stock up for the next season.'

Mahmoud held the lamp high and shone it round. Every-where there were mummies. And now Owen saw, among the crocodiles, mummies which could only be of humans.

'So do you want to go on?' Mahmoud asked again.

'No, thanks,' said Owen. He had the feeling, especially now that he had seen the human mummies, that he was obtruding on someone's privacy.

He said as much to Mahmoud while they were retracing their steps.

Mahmoud was silent for a little while and then said:

'That is why archæology makes me uneasy. I see it adds to knowledge, to history. But it also—'

'Desecrates?' suggested Owen.

As they left, Mahmoud looked carefully again at the place where Miss Skinner had fallen. Then they were on out into the sunlight.

In the courtyard Tomas's men were removing the last parts of the façade.

'But this isn't archæology,' said Mahmoud. 'This is plunder.'

But what, Owen asked himself, was Miss Skinner doing looking at crocodiles? Especially mummified ones?

The Der el Bahari villagers might reasonably wish to augment their stock. Miss Skinner, though, surely, was interested in larger game. She was clearly looking for something; and she was not looking in general, she was looking for something particular. Something which she seemed to know would be there.

It had not been on the list. Or if it had, it had not been on one that Tomas was showing her. Yet the fact that it might have been on the list suggested that it was an object of that sort.

Had Miss Skinner reason to suppose that Parker had found something important, perhaps valuable, that he was anxious to conceal? If it was not on the list, was it not there deliberately? Was Parker going to try to smuggle it out of the country without going through the proper procedures?

And was Miss Skinner anxious to stop him, to catch him publicly in the act? Not so much to expose a malefactor as to expose a system, an inadequacy of procedure—let's say it, of people?

It would look good, wouldn't it: some major find—another Cow of Hathor, perhaps—on the brink of being smuggled out of Egypt, stopped in the nick of time by the efforts of a lone, fearless American woman!

And meanwhile what were the authorities doing? Where, all this time, was the Mamur Zapt, newly given responsibility in this area? Ah, where?

He had actually been *at* Der el Bahari when it all happened. Been there and seen nothing. It had been left to the Lone American Woman to find out what was going on. Had it not been—

Owen decided he didn't like the sound of this at all. It wouldn't read well in the papers. Think of all the fuss there had been over the Cow!

Politically, it wouldn't be that great, either. The rest of the world would pounce on this illustration of English ineptitude and misgovernment, the Nationalists would seize upon it as an example of British connivance in the exploitation of the Egyptian people—

It got worse.

And what could he do about it? He didn't know where the damned thing was, if there was a thing. Or even what it was, unlike Miss Skinner. He could order a search, but what chance was there of finding anything in a warren of a place like this with people like the Der el Bahari villagers who had had centuries of practice at robbing and hiding? It would be down a shaft somewhere and he would never get near it.

The one consolation was that Miss Skinner didn't seem to have found it yet, either.

But he was going away tomorrow and she was staying here and perhaps she would find it the moment he was gone. That would look good, too! The dummo was actually there but left just at the crucial moment!

Ought he to stay?

*

The last two carts were filling up. Tomas's men were bringing the remaining trophies from distant parts of the temple, some of them already boxed up against the journey. Miss Skinner stood by the carts with eagle eye. Tomas, going past, gave a little grimace which only Owen caught.

From inside the temple came a shout and then there was a little commotion. Two of Tomas's men came out supporting a third. He was holding his hand and blood was streaming down.

Owen recognized him. It was the dissident one, the man Mahmoud had talked to, the relative of the dead Abu.

Tomas started across towards him.

'What has happened?' he said.

One of the diggers came out of the temple.

'An accident,' he said.

Tomas sent one of the men for the first-aid kit and bent over the man's hand.

'How did it happen, Idris?' he asked.

'We were moving the sarcophagus,' he said. 'It caught my hand.'

'That all?'

Owen saw a momentary flicker of relief on Tomas's face.

'It's enough, isn't it?' said Idris. 'I've lost my hand.'

'Nonsense!' said Tomas. 'It will be all right in a week or two.'

Idris shook his head.

'Not this,' he said. 'Not this!'

Tomas made him lie back against the wall.

Mahmoud came out of the colonnade.

'What's this?' he said.

'It's your man, Idris. Abu's cousin. He's had an accident.'

'Accident!' said Mahmoud, and went over to the recumbent man.

'Abu?' said Miss Skinner. 'The man who was killed?'

'That's right. They came from the same village.'

The man came running back with the first-aid kit. Someone produced a bowl of water. Tomas began to wash the wound gently. Idris lay back taut-faced.

'I can see the bone,' he said.

'I will cover it up,' said Tomas. 'Tomorrow I will take you to the hakim at Luxor.'

He applied a dressing and then began to bandage. When he had finished, the arm looked as if it had been mummified.

Idris looked at it as if in disbelief.

'This is the end for me,' he said. 'I won't be able to work.'

'You'll be able to work,' said Tomas. 'You'll be able to work in the fields as before.'

'There's no money in the fields.'

'There will be money for you.'

Idris suddenly brightened.

'How much?' he said.

Owen saw Tomas talking to Parker. Parker was off-hand, impatient. He tried to move away. Tomas refused to be shrugged off.

He suggested something to Parker. Parker shook his head. Again he tried to move away. Tomas put out a hand and detained him.

Parker turned on him furiously. Tomas did not give way. For a moment the two men stood toe to toe.

Unexpectedly, it was Parker who appeared to yield. He stepped back, shrugged and turned away. The shrug was one of concession.

Tomas went back to Idris.

'How did it happen, Idris?' asked Mahmoud.

'It tilted,' said Idris. 'I had my hand behind it and it got trapped.'

'How did it come to tilt?'

'I don't know,' said Idris. 'The weight, I suppose. Those things are heavy.'

'Did someone tilt it?'

Idris looked at him, startled.

'It was Ismail,' he said. 'He was on the other side. But he wouldn't have—he's a mate.'

They found Ismail loading something on to the cart. Mahmoud beckoned him over.

'How did it happen, Ismail?' he said.

Ismail was upset.

'I don't know,' he said. 'As God is my witness! I wouldn't have hurt Idris for anything. He's my mate. We've worked together a lot on this job. I wouldn't have hurt him for anything!' He was almost in tears.

'How did it happen, then?'

'I was on the lower end, trying to lift. Only it was too heavy for me. Musa had to help me. He could see I had a job on and he came over to lend me a hand, which was decent of him. Those villagers don't usually stir a finger —'

'Villagers? He's not one of your men, then?'

'No. He's from the village. Which was why I was surprised. But I was glad of his help, I can tell you. Those things are heavy. Too heavy, I suppose. We ought to have had another man on it. But there you are, you don't think of these things until it's too late. Anyway, it just tilted, you see, as we lifted.'

He burst into tears.

'How was I to know Idris had his hand there?'

Musa was short and dark-skinned. He listened to Mahmoud impassively.

'Yes,' he said, 'it tipped over a bit as we got a lift on it. It wasn't done right, you see. The other man should have had his hands up supporting it as we lifted. They shouldn't have been down there! Those men don't know what they're doing.'

'It was his fault, then?'

Musa looked Mahmoud straight in the eye.

'Yes!' he said.

*

'You can't pretend it's my fault,' said Parker. 'Not this time.'

'Three accidents,' said Mahmoud, 'within the space of a month!'

Parker shrugged.

'Sites are dangerous places,' he said. 'These things happen. Tough, but there it is.'

'They shouldn't have been lifting such a big load.'

'Look,' said Parker, 'have you seen these men? They're as strong as donkeys. If you look out of your office in Cairo some time you'll see men carrying pianos. By themselves.'

'I am one of "these men",' said Mahmoud in a fury.

Miss Skinner asked Owen to interpret for her. She asked Idris about Abu's family.

'They are well,' said Idris. 'And, of course, with the money —'

'There was some money?'

'Oh yes. Ten pounds a year. Ten pounds! Tomas says I will get money, too,' said Idris happily. 'If I get ten pounds I will put it towards buying a buffalo and then I shall hire it out and won't have to work so long in the fields.'

'Is it enough,' asked Miss Skinner, 'enough for Abu's family to live on?'

'Barely,' said Owen.

'Then I will make it up,' announced Miss Skinner. 'Can you tell me how I should go about that, please?'

Mahmoud joined them and went over the incident again quietly with Idris. Idris, however, was no longer much interested. His mind was full of the money that would be coming to him. Small though it was, it represented escape, or partial escape, from the fields. He looked upon it as a windfall beside which the injury to his hand was nothing.

'But then,' said Miss Skinner, as they walked across the courtyard, 'he at least has his life. Abu and Rashid lost theirs.'

She stopped and faced Mahmoud.

'Mr el Zaki,' she said, 'you are going to do something, aren't you? You're not going to let them get away with it?'

'There is not enough evidence to convict,' said Mahmoud, shaking his head. 'However . . .'

'My report is an internal matter only,' said Mahmoud. 'However, you will receive notice of the charges.'

'Charges!' said Parker, thunderstruck.

'If, as I expect, we decide to prosecute.'

'Look,' said Parker heavily, tapping Mahmoud on the chest with his forefinger, 'there's no court in the world, not even in Egypt, which would accept a charge of negligence based on that evidence.'

'Who said anything about negligence?'

'Then what—?' Parker stopped, caught off-balance.

'You have clearly breached the terms of your permit,' said Mahmoud, 'and I shall recommend that your licence to excavate be withdrawn.'

'What!' Parker's voice rose in a shout. 'On what grounds?'

'Your licence restricts you to excavation in two places: the sanctuary and the North-East Court.'

'Well?'

'There is evidence of excavation in at least one other place. A breach has been made in the wall of an inner chamber: the chamber, of course, into which Miss Skinner so unfortunately fell. The breach was made recently: in fact, during your occupancy of the site. It can only have been made by you.'

Miss Skinner, intent as ever, watched the last package being loaded on to the cart. Tomas made sure it was fastened correctly and then signalled to the driver. The cart rumbled off in a cloud of dust.

Through the dust Owen could see the guide approaching

with the riding mules. There were four of them: one each for himself and Mahmoud and the other two—?

'You will, after all, have the pleasure of my company,' said Miss Skinner.

CHAPTER 8

Back in his office, Owen found that little had occurred in his absence. The heat inhibited crime as it did any other kind of activity. The city seemed positively deserted. The poor were asleep and the rich on holiday.

Most well-to-do Cairenes took their families to Alexandria for the summer, where they could enjoy the cool sea breezes of the coast. Many British, including the Consul-General, did likewise. For a month or two it was as if the centre of gravity of Egypt had shifted northwards.

So it was perhaps not surprising that the only thing which seemed to require Owen's attention should emanate from Alexandria. Fortunately, it was extremely minor: a request from some Italian businessmen to be allowed to erect a statue of Dante in one of the squares.

Owen, glad to be back in Cairo and feeling benign to all the world, even, this morning, the Finance Department, was about to accede to this request when his eye caught a scribbled note in the margin from the Consul-General no less: 'Suggest you go and see them.'

Well, this was all right, too. A quick trip up to Alexandria, snatch some of the sea breezes, catch a late train back . . . Perhaps even go to the Opera?

He suggested it to Zeinab.

'Travelling all day there and all night back? On a train? In this heat?' She shook her head. 'Not even to go to the Opera.'

So he went alone, sitting comfortably by himself, watching the green fields and brown earth of the delta go by, with the fellahin stooping in the gadwals and the little boys perched on top of their buffaloes.

Alexandria was noticeably fuller of visitors than it had been even a few days ago, but with its wide streets, open squares and French-style parks and public gardens it seemed easily able to accommodate them all.

It was indeed a European, not an Arab, city. The streets were well laid out, with the houses, in this part of the city, well apart. Broad, open lawns stretched up to sunny walls covered with a blaze of creepers. The gardens were open to the street in front. All was well watered and to Owen's eye, still adjusting from the harsh glare of the desert, almost stridently green.

His arabeah pulled up outside one of the houses. A short, plump Italian in a dark suit and a red fez rushed out, took both his hands in his and drew him into the house and through into an inner garden.

Two men were sitting at a table drinking lemonade. They jumped up as they saw him and came towards him with effusive Italian warmth.

'So good of you! So good!'

Their French was better than their English. In Alexandria English took third place to French and Italian. Owen had no Italian, so after a moment or two's exploring they all shifted naturally into French.

'You have not been to Italy?'

Owen had to confess that he hadn't.

'Ah, you should!'

'I should, too,' said one of the men, laughing.

'You are not . . . ?' said Owen, surprised.

'I'm Italian all right,' the man said, 'but I've never been in Italy. I was born in Alexandria.'

'He's an Alexandrian,' said one of the others. 'I am, too, but not from birth. Not quite. My parents came here when I was three years old.'

'But you are still Italian?'

'Italian *and* Alexandrian.'

They seemed happy to be, proud of being, both. Italian was what they thought of themselves as, but Alexandria was where they had always lived and where they expected always to live.

'You shift your roots,' said one of the men, 'and then you grow them again. You still remember your roots but now they are in different soil.'

Owen suddenly thought that that was his case, too. It was over twelve years since he had last been in England, but he still thought of it as home. In fact, he had no home there. His parents were dead, his relatives few and scattered. He no longer kept in touch with them. Egypt was his home, if he had one, the place where he had put down roots.

But you never quite shook your origins off. You took, as one of the Italians said, bits of your home country with you.

'Opera,' said Owen.

Their faces lit up.

'Verdi.'

'Puccini.'

He told them he had seen the current production of *The Mastersingers* at the Zizinia.

'Hmm.' They weren't too sure about that. 'But tonight there is *Tosca!*'

Owen laughed.

'Well, perhaps I shall see it,' he said.

'In that case we shall see you,' they said, pleased.

But opera was not the only thing the Italians had brought with them to Alexandria. The restaurants were Italian, Italian was the language of the shops. And if intellectual allegiance in Cairo was owed to France, in Alexandria, so the Italians claimed, it was owed to the country of Michelangelo, Da Vinci and Bernini.

Hence Dante.

'A tribute,' they said, 'to the great poet of the Mediterranean.'

They wished to erect a statue in one of the squares.

'Nothing out of the ordinary,' they said. 'About six feet high. Standing on a simple block. Well done, of course.'

And they would pay for it. That, Owen thought, was probably the clincher. The British Administration in Egypt, like the British Government at home, was not against art, even on occasions for it, provided that somebody else paid.

He said he did not think there would be any problem.

'Order?' asked one of the Italians tentatively. 'Public order?'

'Order? A statue of Dante? I don't see why.'

'Oh, good, then.'

They parted, the Italians saying they would look out for him at the Zizinia that night.

In fact, he met someone else there he knew: Carmichael, the man from Customs.

'Hello,' said Carmichael, 'come down to see us again?'

'Not this time,' said Owen. He told Carmichael about the statue.

'Ah!' said Carmichael. 'The statue! Been a lot in the papers about it.'

'Really? Well,' said Owen, looking around him and fired for the moment with enthusiasm for things Italian, 'it seems a nice idea.'

'Yes,' said Carmichael, a little doubtfully. Then, more positively—he was, after all, an opera-goer himself—'yes.'

He was, however, also a member of the British Administration.

'Of course, the Moslems don't think so.'

'Don't think so?'

'No. They're opposed to it. As a matter of fact, they're dead against it.'

'But why? A statue of a poet—?'

'A heathen statue. That's how the clerics see it. And then, of course, the Nationalists have jumped on the bandwagon. Another foreigner. Whose country is this? Why should a foreigner be honoured? Etcetera, etcetera. It's a real *cause célèbre* down here, I can tell you.'

'I see,' said Owen, who now did.

'Glad you're handling it. Rather you than me, old man.'

In a box opposite he saw the girl he had met in the Customs, the one in the green coat with the ape-god. It was just a glimpse as she disappeared into one of the enclosed harem boxes. The Italians were as jealous of their women as the Moslems were.

He saw her again, however, at the interval. She was standing with an elderly, grey-haired man and also with one of the Italians he had spoken to that afternoon, who caught his eye and waved him over.

'Signor Seppi. Francesca.'

'We've met,' said the girl.

'Captain Owen. The Mamur Zapt.'

'Ah!' said the girl. 'I didn't know that.'

Again he felt the cool touch of her hand.

'Captain Owen is supporting us over the statue.'

'I am sympathetic,' said Owen. 'That, however, is all.'

The man looked at him wryly.

'Ah!' he said. 'You have found out.'

'I am still sympathetic.'

'We shall keep working on you.'

'I can see that you like to combine business with pleasure,' said Francesca, looking around her.

'I always come to the Zizinia when I am in Alexandria.'

'And I always go to the Opera House when I am in Cairo.'

'You are often in Cairo?'

'Business. I go to the Museum regularly.'

'Francesca handles that side for me,' said Signor Seppi,

looking at her fondly, 'now that I can no longer get around.'

He was, Owen now saw, older than he looked. He had one of those fine Mediterranean faces which seemed to remain young, but the body was frail and the hands old and mottled.

'Francesca never ceases to amaze me,' said the other Italian. 'Such energy! In this heat!'

'She is a son to me,' declared the old man, 'and has been since Paulo died.'

'I couldn't leave you to run the business on your own, could I?' said the girl, touching him gently on the arm.

'I admire your determination,' said Owen. 'It cannot be easy in a country like this.'

The girl shrugged.

'Roberto had built up the business. And then Paulo. All I had to do was to carry it on.'

'All the same . . .'

'She is a true Italian,' said Signor Seppi, 'like her mother. In our part of Italy there is a saying: "When the men die, the women have to do the work."'

'I deal mostly with Europeans,' said Francesca. 'Pashas as well, of course, but I don't usually deal with them directly.'

'You have Pashas among your clients?'

'Increasingly.'

'She deals only with the best,' said Signor Seppi proudly.

'Buying or selling?' asked Owen.

The girl looked at him sharply.

'Both.'

'You are interested in antiquities, Monsieur?' asked Signor Seppi.

The girl laughed.

'Captain Owen's interest is, I suspect, purely professional,' she said.

'Not entirely,' said Owen. 'I am fond of things Italian.'

The girl smiled.

*

The Khedivial Sports Club, or Gezira, as it was known, was the principal social centre for the British Administration in Cairo. It would have been charming anyway even if it had had no sports because it was like an English park and reminded people of home. It had broad stretches of turf, lovely southern trees and marvellous flowers.

But it had also all kinds of sport going on within its precincts: cricket and polo at the usual hours and golf, tennis and croquet while daylight lasted.

It had also a clubhouse, run on much the same principles as those at Ranelagh, the home-from-home of young English officers when they were based in England. Young officers when they were posted in Egypt, and there were a lot of young British officers posted to Egypt, found it easy to transfer their allegiance. They were able to carry on their sport, drinking and betting on horses exactly as they had done in England.

It was, Owen supposed, the British equivalent of the Italians importing their Opera.

Anyway, it was a very nice place to go and picnic beneath the trees and watch the races and the sport, and on afternoons when there were major engagements most of the British community in Egypt could be found there.

The engagement this afternoon, however, was a little out of the ordinary and had attracted an even larger crowd than usual. The usual racing fraternity were there and all the young officers. But there was, too, a considerable sprinkling of notables. The Consul-General himself was present, most of the foreign diplomats, many of the great Pashas and even, it was whispered, Royalty.

There was, too, on the far side of the trees, where the sand crept up to and touched the green, what was even more unusual: a considerable crowd of Arabs, many of them Bedawin on camels.

For this was, actually, a camel occasion. Garvin, the

Commandant of the Cairo Police, was putting a camel over the steeplechase course.

Ordinarily, camels do not jump. Some, after training, will stumble in their gallop over a two-foot obstacle. But this particular camel jumped like a horse.

Garvin had recently acquired him from a member of the Sudan Survey. The camel came from the Bayuda desert to the south of the Fourth Cataract in the Sudan and no one had yet seen him up in these parts.

They had, however, heard of him. The fame of Abu Rusas, 'father of bullets', had spread far and wide. The camel owed his name to having been hit as a colt by the bullet of some raiding Dervishes who were trying to capture him, and which had left him with a hernia that stuck out like a tennis ball from his belly and made him difficult to girth.

Abu Rusas was famous for his running but now it appeared he had developed a new talent: steeplechasing. Garvin had been fostering it in secret for some time and was now prepared to go public.

There was a steeplechase course of natural hedges alongside the flat course at the Gezira and it was over this that Garvin now proposed to put him.

When Owen arrived with Zeinab, Garvin was just taking Abu Rusas down the course to have a preliminary look at the obstacles. Garvin was riding the camel himself. He was a very good rider, both of horses and camels, having ridden a lot of the latter in his days in the Camel Patrol.

Owen had ridden camel and horse in his time in the Army but did not reckon himself a rider in the sense that Garvin was. Garvin was the son of a country 'squarson', squire-parson, and had grown up to huntin', shootin' and fishin'.

Owen was the son of a clergyman, too, but his father had been a poor, bookish Anglican vicar in a Welsh, predominantly Nonconformist parish. There was no hunting and shooting round there! The young officers had Garvin's background rather than his. It was one of the things that had made him feel out of place in the Army in India, one of the things that had led him to transfer to the civil administration in Egypt.

He was present on this occasion chiefly as a fellow-policeman, giving Garvin moral support. Zeinab was there not because she was interested in horses and racing—like Owen, she was very much a city person—but because the freakishness of the spectacle had caught her imagination. In this almost exclusively European context she had discarded her veil; and her Arab features attracted some curious glances from the English families as she walked past with Owen.

They arrived at the course at the same time as Paul and Miss Skinner.

'You will find this very interesting, Miss Skinner,' Paul was saying.

'Bizarre, certainly,' said Miss Skinner. She looked round and saw Zeinab.

'Why, Miss Nuri,' she said, putting out her hand and cheering up, 'this is fortunate. Now that I am back in Cairo I was thinking of giving you call.'

'A pleasure!' beamed Zeinab. She placed Miss Skinner in the same exotic category as jumping camels.

The two ladies stood together as Garvin brought Abu Rusas back to the starting-line.

Over on the other side of the course, in front of the assembled Arabs, a few motor-cars had drawn up on to the grass. They were still unusual in Cairo and attracted almost as much attention as Abu Rusas. Their owners, wealthy Pashas for the most part, sat on folding chairs in front of them. Several had brought massive hampers. This was clearly a festive occasion.

One of the chair-holders waved his hand.

'It is my father,' said Zeinab. 'Perhaps we will go and talk to him afterwards.'

For the event was about to begin. Garvin touched the side of the camel's neck with his heel and the great beast moved off at the trot. As they came up to the first obstacle, the trot accelerated to a gallop and then Abu Rusas was flying over the hedge like a bird.

The onlookers broke into loud applause.

'Incredible!'

'Bravo!'

'Bismillah!'

'Inshallah! God is mighty!'

And then Abu Rusas was speeding down the course, taking the hedges with the aplomb of the favourite at the Grand National.

At the far end Garvin pulled up in triumph and then came trotting sedately back, acknowledging the cheers. Even Miss Skinner was impressed.

'My goodness!' she said.

The people who were most impressed, however, were the Arabs on camels opposite, who thought they knew something about camels. Several of them were known to Garvin from his earlier days patrolling the desert and when he reached the end of the course he rode over to them to exchange expert notes.

'Shall we go over to your father?' asked Owen.

'Do come,' Zeinab said to Miss Skinner. 'My father will be glad to see you.'

That appeared an understatement as Nuri rose from his chair, clasped Miss Skinner's hand in his and led her to a chair hurriedly put beside him, giving Zeinab merely an acknowledging gleam of his eye.

'We will have a picnic!' declared Nuri, waving one hand enthusiastically. The other continued to hold Miss Skinner's hand firmly.

Servants spread a car rug for Zeinab, Owen and Paul and

opened a bottle of champagne. Nuri, still loosely Moslem, in public at any rate, was not a great drinker but he believed in coming provided.

Paul raised his glass to someone in front of a neighbouring car.

'Marbrouk,' he said, 'the old scoundrel.'

'The Pasha Marbrouk?' said Miss Skinner.

'I will introduce you to him,' said Nuri.

The Pasha Marbrouk, equally well provided, joined his campsite to Nuri's. They were old Government colleagues, which meant, of course, that they were rivals.

'*Chère Madame!*' said Marbrouk, raising Miss Skinner's hand to his lips.

Nuri looked displeased. Hospitality was not intended to extend so far.

Once or twice during the conversation Marbrouk's eyes strayed in Zeinab's direction. Zeinab, caught without her veil, stirred awkwardly.

Owen felt displeased also. Between old politicians, even rivals, there was always the possibility of attempts to strike unexpected deals and family alliances were sometimes the cement.

'We have only just returned from your estate, Mr Marbrouk,' said Miss Skinner.

'My estate?' Marbrouk raised his eyebrows. 'Which one?'

'Der el Bahari.'

'Ah, that!' Marbrouk dismissed it with a wave of his hand. 'But that is nothing. Backward! And so hot at this time of year! Come to El Howeini, Miss Skinner. That is far nicer. Yes, do come. I would be delighted to show you my orange groves.'

'I would be more interested,' said Miss Skinner, 'in seeing your famous collection of antiquities.'

'Ah yes,' said Marbrouk. His eyes hooded, just for the moment, so that he seemed suddenly like a great, sleek bird of prey. 'But for that,' he said, smiling, 'we don't need to go all the way to El Howeini. Many of my treasures are in my house here, in Cairo.'

'I would be most interested,' said Miss Skinner.

'Although, of course, the majority are at my house in Heraq.'

'Heraq?' said Miss Skinner. 'Is that on the river?'

'Almost everything in Egypt is on the river,' said Marbrouk, smiling.

'Yes,' said Miss Skinner, 'yes, I should like to come to Heraq.'

'I have treasures, too,' said Nuri, giving her hand a squeeze.

Miss Skinner gave him an encouraging smile.

'I would love to see them, too.'

'Then that is settled,' said Marbrouk. 'In a day or two, perhaps?'

Nuri was relieved to see him go.

Garvin brought Abu Rusas over to them.

'Congratulations!' said Miss Skinner. 'A most remarkable spectacle.'

'The grass was a bit slippery,' said Garvin. 'That was the only problem, really.'

He walked Abu Rusas round them, drawing admiring cries from the Arabs behind.

'May I stroke him?' asked Miss Skinner, disengaging her hand from Nuri's.

'Probably best not. They're not used to that sort of thing.'

As if in confirmation, Abu Rusas stirred slightly.

Garvin looked up at the line of Arabs on their camels and said something in Arabic. The Arabs laughed and the line parted. A camel backed out.

It was a huge camel, as big as Abu Rusas himself. It seemed to be blowing a bubble, a disgusting, large, pink bubble as big as a balloon, hanging like chewing-gum, bubble-gum, from the side of its mouth.

Abu Rusas lurched threateningly and the rider of the other camel hastily turned it away.

'Is something wrong with it?' asked Miss Skinner.

'Not at all, my dear Miss Skinner,' said Nuri, shocked. 'Rather the reverse! It means that it is in rut. Ready,' he said, seizing her hand happily, 'to mate.'

'But where,' asked Miss Skinner, 'is the leopard, the dear little leopard?'

'Leopard?' said Tomas, taken aback.

They were at the Museum, in the large room downstairs. All around them were what Miss Skinner kept referring to as 'the Spoils of Der el Bahari'. There were the boxes Owen had watched being loaded on to the carts, there the lotus-wreathed pediments and there the pieces of façade.

'You remember?' Miss Skinner said to Owen. 'The Expedition to Punt. The dear little leopard being led on board? At least, I hope it was a dear little one and not a big one.'

'Why, yes,' said Owen, 'I remember.'

'Where is it?'

'It must be here somewhere,' said Tomas.

He had arrived with the packages that morning. Owen had asked to be kept informed as to when the packages were being delivered. He had wanted to see the whole process. The under-keeper had told him they were being delivered that day. He had gone along first thing and had been a little surprised to find Miss Skinner already there.

And in form. She had, it appeared, taken matters out of the under-keeper's hands and was checking through the items herself.

'Something missing?' said the under-keeper.

'No,' said Tomas. 'I checked it all through yesterday.'

'Perhaps it was left at Heraq?'

'No,' said Tomas. 'I counted everything on to the boat. And then again at the docks. And here.'

'Well, where is it, then?' asked Miss Skinner.

Tomas began checking the individual pieces of façade. 'Is this it?'

'No,' said Miss Skinner. 'Apes, yes, but not a leopard.'

'Here is a leopard!'

'Yes,' said Miss Skinner, inspecting it, 'but not *the* leopard. A dear little baby cub being led on board. Captain Owen remembers it clearly.'

'Yes,' said Owen, 'I do.'

'You said you had brought the complete façade,' the under-keeper said to Tomas. 'We could try fitting the pieces together and see if one is missing.'

'It's not the complete façade,' said Tomas touchily. 'It's only a part of it. The part that covers the Expedition.'

'Well, we could still see if it fitted.'

'Yes,' said Tomas, rather surlily, 'we could.'

'I don't think any other piece has gone missing,' said Miss Skinner, 'apart from that. But I remember the leopard cub particularly.'

'It will be somewhere,' Tomas said to the under-keeper. 'Why don't you carry on with the other pieces and then we can look for that afterwards.'

'Yes,' said the under-keeper. 'We'll be able to see what we've got left.'

'By all means,' said Miss Skinner. 'Only don't forget about it at the end. I am particularly anxious to see what happens to my little leopard.'

'It's obviously impressed you,' said the under-keeper. 'I'd like to see it, too.'

'It will be here somewhere,' said Tomas.

However, it wasn't.

'Fallen off the back of a cart?' suggested Miss Skinner, her face expressionless.

CHAPTER 9

Or off the back of a boat, Owen said to himself. Where was that port Tomas said he took the things to before assembling them together to go to the Museum? Wasn't that Heraq, too? It was time he went to Heraq.

There were several small ports on the southern side of the city, but Heraq, if he remembered rightly, was several miles further on upstream, not part of the city at all. It would take about half a day to get there and he would have to go by boat.

His day brightened at the thought. He would take a felucca, one of those small, graceful river craft which skimmed over the surface of the Nile like a bird and would do the journey in a couple of hours. He would loll back in the stern and enjoy the river breeze.

That seemed a particularly good idea this morning as he sat in his airless office in the sweltering heat. Normally, Der el Bahari was so much hotter than Cairo that on his return to the city he would have found it pleasantly mild.

He seemed, however, to have brought the heat back with him. The temperature in Cairo had suddenly risen and the cabmen, as he had left the station, were complaining bitterly. He had arrived in the evening, which was fortunate as otherwise he wouldn't have found any cabmen at all. By about ten in the morning the heat was so overwhelming that the streets were deserted. Everyone downed tools and returned to the shade and complained.

Except, of course, in the Bab el Khalk, where the British affected to be impervious to the heat and the great fans whirled continuously and the sweat ran down your arms and on to the papers on your desk, making them unpleasantly soggy. The ink ran and the edges of the papers turned and within about half an hour you needed to change your shirt.

Yes, it would be nice to be on the river.

'I shall be going to Heraq,' he informed his clerk, hesitated between sun helmet and tarboosh, chose the sun helmet—the tarboosh was a thing of the city—and went out.

What he had overlooked in his pleasant vision was that for the first four miles of the journey upstream the river ran between steep levees, mudbanks of silt which over the centuries had built up to such an extent that it was like sailing between walls.

If you were sitting on the top deck of one of Mr Cook's new steamers you might be able to see something of the surrounding countryside. Down on the waterline, as you were in a felucca, all you could see were the tops of the palms.

Still, there was the breeze and he happily made the most of it.

After a while the levees dropped and he was able to see something. Over to his left was a mountain of white stone on which he could see the occasional puff. This was the quarry of Tura, which produced the fine limestone which faced Chephren's pyramid. In Chephren's time it had been on the river. Now it was half a mile away.

The river began to pass through plantations of date palms and lines of delicate green tamarisks. There was a huge dovecote with massive mud walls and domes and minarets and little ledges for the birds. There were donkeys and women washing clothes and men moulding mud bricks.

And then the trees fell away and there was a cluster of mud brick buildings and a brickyard beside a wharf. The felucca turned in.

'Heraq,' said the boatman.

Owen was a little surprised. He had expected a working port—that, after all, was why he was there—but he had also expected something a bit more rural. Hadn't Marbrouk said his estate was there? This was almost industrial. There were piles of mud bricks waiting to be loaded and on beyond the main wharf another one for loading the limestone from the quarry.

He stepped out of the felucca and asked one of the men working where the main warehouse was.

'Warehouse?' said the man. He pointed to the bricks and the stone. 'We don't need one.'

'What about when the antiquities come?'

The man didn't understand him.

'When Tomas brings his things.'

'Tomas?'

The workman called across to some men piling mud bricks.

'The Pasha's man, isn't he?' one of them said.

'A Copt,' said Owen, though they would know that from the name.

A man came out from behind the wall of piled bricks.

'Here, Ali,' they said, 'he wants to know about the Pasha's man.'

'Why?' said the man.

Owen found the question unexpectedly hard to answer. He could invoke authority, but here out of Cairo the Pasha was the one with the authority.

'He thinks he's left one of the things behind,' he said.

'Well, that's easy enough,' said the man. 'There were plenty of them.'

He turned on his heel and led Owen up behind the bricks to a beaten earth square in which there were sacks of dates and packages of various kinds. Leaning against the wall were some of the objects from Der el Bahari: among them the piece of façade with the leopard cub.

'That's it,' said Owen.

The man shrugged.

'I expect someone thought it was meant to go up to the house with the others,' he said.

'Why, Captain Owen,' said a familiar voice behind him. 'I see you've found our dear little leopard.'

Miss Skinner had just come into the yard with Marbrouk and, somewhat to Owen's surprise, Nuri.

Miss Skinner came up to him.

'It's lovely, isn't it?' she said, looking at the façade. 'Captain Owen and I both remarked this dear little cub,' she said, turning to Marbrouk. 'That was at Der el Bahari. We looked for it at Cairo. I dare say it's on its way, is it?'

Marbrouk stepped forward and inspected it.

'A fine piece of work,' he said. 'Yes, it's on its way.'

'Is it on the list?' asked Owen.

'The façade is certainly on the list,' said Miss Skinner. 'Of course, the fragments are not listed individually. One just has to be sure that they all get there,' she added, smiling. 'Doesn't one?'

'It should have gone with the other pieces,' said Marbrouk. 'An oversight. I'll see it is sent on. These people! You can never rely on them.'

'I thought Tomas was pretty reliable,' said Owen.

'He's all right,' said Marbrouk. 'He's probably arranged for these to follow separately for some reason.'

'I'm so glad,' said Miss Skinner. 'Captain Owen has become quite attached to that little leopard.'

'Why don't you come up to the house,' said Marbrouk, 'and have some refreshment?'

'I don't want to interrupt you,' said Owen.

'I was just showing Miss Skinner around the estate. This bit is not very pleasant. But it makes money.'

'I prefer the orange groves,' said Miss Skinner.

They walked back to the house. It lay among orange groves and date plantations and was completely shielded from the dock. It was a large, single-storey, white, mud brick house built around a courtyard in which a fountain was playing. The courtyard was like a Greek or a Turkish garden, densely packed with shrubs for shade. The scent of oleander hung heavily in the air.

They sat down beside the fountain and servants brought them lemonade and dates and little sweet, sticky cakes.

'You see I have been taking Mr Marbrouk up on his kind offer,' said Miss Skinner.

'And did you find his treasures interesting?'

'Oh, most interesting. Most interesting.'

'I would like to see them, too, if I may,' said Owen.

'Of course,' said the Pasha, but remained seated.

'I have fine treasures, too,' Nuri said to Miss Skinner. 'You must come and see mine.'

Guessing, perhaps, that Owen was puzzled by Nuri's presence, Miss Skinner said:

'When I asked Mr Nuri how to get here he very kindly offered to drive me here in his car.'

'A pleasure,' said Nuri, smiling sweetly at Marbrouk.

Marbrouk did not reciprocate.

'It is so nice,' said Miss Skinner, 'to see inside people's houses. It really helps me to feel I'm getting to know the country.'

'This is just a weekend retreat,' said Marbrouk. 'I come up here with a friend or two when I need privacy. A special friend, of course.'

'Of course,' said Miss Skinner, smiling encouragingly.

They left shortly afterwards. Nuri did not offer Owen a lift. As he shook hands with Marbrouk, he said:

'So glad we've been able to have a word about that other thing, too. It's been in my mind for some time.'

'Yes,' said Marbrouk, brightening. 'Yes.' He had appeared rather cast down.

'I'm so glad we were able to locate that leopard,' Owen said to Miss Skinner.

For a moment Miss Skinner seemed startled.

'Leopard?'

She seemed to have forgotten all about it. Then she remembered.

'Oh, yes. Our dear little cub. Though I'm sure it would have caught up with us later.'

The car drove off. Owen half expected Marbrouk to invite him in. Instead, he shook him firmly by the hand.

'Goodbye, old chap,' he said. '*Bon voyage!*'

Owen retraced his steps through the plantations, glad of the shade. As he emerged into the heat of the port he saw, standing on the wharf where the stone was loaded, a figure he recognized. It was the Italian girl from Alexandria, Francesca.

She looked up at him, surprised.

'We meet again,' she said, putting out her hand. 'I did not expect so soon.'

'But what brings you to a place like this?'

'The stone,' she said, with a gesture. 'We need some occasionally for our workshops. I like to choose it myself because it has to be good quality. They know what I'm looking for and put some aside for me. But what are you doing here?'

'I'm looking for a leopard.'

He took her into the yard and showed her the sculpture.

'It's lovely,' she said. 'But isn't it part of something bigger. I've seen it before. Isn't it . . . The temple at Der el Bahari! The Expedition to Punt!'

'That's right. At Der el Bahari no longer.'

'That is a shame. It seemed so right there. Of course in the Museum more people will see it.'

'If it gets there.'

'If it gets there?'

He indicated the leopard.

'Oh, I see. And that's why you're here, of course.'

'And then it might not stay in the Museum.'

'True. But then, the country needs the money.'

'The country may. I'm not sure all the individuals do.'
She laughed.

'I don't think I'd better enter into that discussion. Especially as I'm just going to see the Pasha Marbrouk.'

'Really? What—?' He stopped.

'About the stone,' she said reprovingly.

'He handles the business side himself?'

'No.' The idea amused her. 'I think,' she said drily, 'it may be because he fancies other things besides antiquities. But weren't you saying that recently about yourself?'

Paul rang up mid-morning to ask if Owen could get over to the Consulate-General immediately. Since he had to get there by arabeah, the answer was no; but he arrived soon after.

He found Paul talking to Abu Bakir, the tall Egyptian he had met in the discussion with Peripoulin about the export of antiquities. They had, apparently, been following up the licence idea.

'And then Abu Bakir raised this —'

'In passing,' said the Egyptian hurriedly.

'—and I thought that as you had actually been there at the time, it might be worth having a little private discussion. It's the Parker business. The two accidents.'

'I wasn't there at the time. It was afterwards. You were, too.'

'You were there during the investigation, that's the point,' said Abu Bakir.

'What's the problem?'

'Mr el Zaki's approach has been challenged.'

'Ignore Parker.'

'It's not so much Parker, it's—well, it's higher up.'

He did say he had friends, thought Owen.

'How high up? And where? In the Ministry?'

Abu Bakir hesitated.

'Leaning on the Ministry,' said Paul.

'What exactly is the issue?'

'Mr el Zaki recommended that the licence to excavate be withdrawn. It is that recommendation that is being challenged. On the grounds that Mr el Zaki was biased'.

'I was there,' said Owen. 'I would be prepared to testify that Mr el Zaki's approach was entirely in order.'

He suddenly remembered, however, some of the exchanges between Parker and Mahmoud.

'Oh, good,' said Abu Bakir, clearly relieved.

'Parker is a bastard.'

Paul tapped a pencil on the writing-pad he had in front of him.

'It's not so much the particular question of Parker himself, though, incidentally, I agree with you. It is, I'm afraid, the more general question.'

'What general question?'

'Of bias against foreigners.'

'Oh, that's ridiculous!' said Owen, 'Come on, Paul: you know Mahmoud yourself!'

'Of course I know Mahmoud. And of course I know it's ridiculous. But, you see, the issue then becomes different.'

'Why does it become different?'

'Because it relates to the Administration's own attitudes. To its policy, if you like.'

'Does the Government welcome foreign investment?' said Abu Bakir. 'Or does it wish to discourage it?'

'This isn't investment,' said Owen. 'It's bloody robbery!'

Abu Bakir roared with laughter.

'You'd better not testify to that!' he said.

'That's the thing we're trying to stop,' said Paul. 'What we don't want to stop, though, is *bona fide* excavation. Especially with other people's money.'

'It's mostly American money these days,' said Abu Bakir. 'That's the point, really.'

'Can't you make a distinction between *bona fide* excavation and Parker's sort of stripping?' asked Owen.

'The Americans don't know the difference,' said Paul, with Oxford superciliousness.

Abu Bakir smiled.

'It's not that easy,' he said. 'Parker probably does some genuine work as well as the stripping. It's the price we have to pay.'

'It's a question of proportion,' said Paul. 'Parker goes too far. Other people have got more sense. Or less greed. The trouble is, it's hard to draw an administrative line beforehand. You rely on people's judgement.'

'Anyway,' said Abu Bakir, 'that, strictly speaking, isn't the issue. The issue is the accidents, or at least the investigation into them.'

'It's not even that, strictly speaking,' said Paul. 'Mahmoud was unable to establish a basis for pressing a charge on the grounds of negligence. What he got him on was exceeding the terms of his licence.'

'The counter-argument,' said Abu Bakir, who seemed to know a lot about it, 'is that this was a minor breach of conditions and that Mr el Zaki was being over-zealous in recommending withdrawal of the licence to excavate.'

'And also,' said Paul, 'that this over-zealousness proceeds from a general bias against foreigners and that if action is not taken against him, then this will be taken as evidence of the Government's general attitude in such matters.'

'Mahmoud gets disciplined and Parker gets away with it?'

Paul nodded.

'That's about right.'

'I think if the Government did take that view, it would be challenged in the Assembly,' said Abu Bakir.

Paul looked at Owen.

'Abu Bakir speaks with authority.'

'Not authority,' the Egyptian quietly protested. 'Knowledge of the probabilities, say.'

'Good knowledge of the probabilities,' said Paul, smiling.

Owen remembered Abu Bakir's Nationalist sympathies.

'So either way . . .' said Paul.

We have a political problem, thought Owen. If the Nationalists took that line, they would be able to stir up a lot of trouble. It would be fertile ground for the cultivation of anti-foreign feeling, which could easily spill over into other areas.

What was worse was that other countries might well feel some sympathy with the Nationalist view and use the issue to exert pressure on Britain to abandon its privileged position in Egypt. Other countries, *most* other countries, would be only too anxious to prise Britain out of Egypt.

'You see,' said Paul.

Abu Bakir was watching them carefully.

What was *his* motivation, Owen wondered. Why had he come to Paul? Why, if he was such a Nationalist, had he not just gone ahead, let the issue blow up and then exploited it in the Assembly? Why go to Paul?

'Tell me,' he said to Abu Bakir, 'who is it exactly who is putting pressure on the Ministry?'

'Foreign interests,' said Abu Bakir.

'Directly?'

There was a little pause.

'Not exactly directly,' Abu Bakir admitted.

'Indirectly, then. Through others?'

'Yes.'

'Who are the others?'

Abu Bakir shrugged his shoulders. 'The usual ones.'

'The Khedive?'

'Not directly,' the Egyptian conceded.

'Indirectly, again? Through intermediaries?'

Abu Bakir nodded.

'I think we need to know the names of the intermediaries,' said Owen.

'I don't know their names. They'll be the usual ones. The great Pashas—'

'Are you sure? This is important.'

'It's always the Pashas in the end, in a thing like this, isn't it?' said Abu Bakir bitterly.

Behind the front of a popular legislative Assembly, behind the façade of Cabinet Government, Egypt was still a feudal country. The Pashas were its great barons, holding most of the land, employing most of the people outside the big cities, jostling for positions of favour with the Khedive, intriguing, constantly intriguing, to get their hands on the levers of power.

Even the British had not been able to dislodge them. Perhaps they did not try too much. Used to them, seeing them, perhaps, as the equivalent of the great English families which had dominated English politics until very recently, the Administration was content to coexist. So long as it could do what it wanted within its sphere, it was content that the Pashas should do what they wished within theirs.

It would take a revolution to sweep them away. Which was, of course, what the new Nationalist Party was saying.

'Is it all the Pashas?' asked Owen. 'Or just some of them?'

'It will be just some of them,' said Paul, 'on something like this.'

'Those who have a particular interest, perhaps,' said Owen, 'in the export of antiquities?'

Owen had to go and see Finance. He knew what it was about; he had mislaid a trifling sum, well, three thousand piastres, actually, and Finance wanted to know where it was.

Owen knew where it was. It was in the hands of various gentlemen in the Silversmiths' Bazaar, the Shoemakers' Bazaar and the Sudanese Bazaar; and it was there for services rendered.

Why was payment not made against a proper invoice? Because these gentlemen were not the sort to send invoices.

And because the services they had rendered were not exactly the kind of thing you sent invoices for.

Could he at least specify the services?

Oh yes. Bribing various camel-herders to reveal what else they carried besides dates; offering inducements to the servants in the Khedive's uncle's palace in order to ascertain the connection between the uncle and the slave trade in the Sudan; suborning a kavass in one of the Legations to provide evidence of the relation between some of the Legation's activities and the traffic in drugs. He could name the Legation—

Perhaps better not. And perhaps it was better not to mention the Khedive's relations. And that bit about bribes . . .

The trouble was that the Accounts went back to England, where they were crawled over by a committee of high-minded MPs who shared the new Liberal Government's distrust of imperial adventure and were prone to unexpected fits of morality.

Better, he had found, to say nothing, or as little as he could. And so he had included the three thousand piastres under a broad heading of 'General Expenditure'; which was, unfortunately, a little too general for the Finance Department's liking.

He knew how it would go; and did not hasten his steps.

When he got there it was as he feared.

'Look, old chap, we can't have this,' said the Finance man, tapping the page of accounts with the end of his pen. 'I mean, three thousand piastres! No invoices. Audit would have our blood. We've got to have details.'

'It's a bit tricky—' Owen was beginning, when a door at the other end of the room opened and a voice shouted: 'Clayton!'

The man opposite rose hurriedly from his chair.

'Shan't be a moment,' he said.

He was gone, however, for twenty minutes and then

emerged pink-faced and at a run. He was carrying an armful of ledgers, which he put down on the desk of one of the clerks. He said something tersely and then was heading back into the other room when Owen intercepted him.

'How long are you going to be?'

'Christ knows! It's that bloody woman again!'

'Well, I'm not sitting here all morning,' Owen pointed out.

'Sorry, old chap, it'll have to be some other time.'

Clayton rushed off.

Owen sat for a moment nursing his wrath.

'Can you handle this?' he said to one of the clerks. The clerk glanced at it.

'Sorry, effendi,' he said. 'It's a policy decision.'

Owen got to his feet.

'I'm making a policy decision, too,' he said. 'Tell Clayton he can bloody well come to me next time. That's if he wants to see me.'

He stalked out. On the way he passed the door to the other office. Inside he saw Miss Skinner. She was surrounded by files and perspiring Finance people.

'Surely you have records?' she was saying.

'I think they may be at Alexandria,' one of the perspirers said.

'May be?' said Miss Skinner cuttingly. 'Don't you know?'

'They're probably still in the Douane. Things get delayed,' said the man sulkily.

Miss Skinner turned some papers over.

'These are dated three years ago,' she pointed out. 'Still in the Douane?'

Serves the so-and-so right, thought Owen with grim satisfaction, and continued on past. He was just going down the stairs when a thought struck him. He hesitated, thought again and then retraced his steps.

'Why, it's Captain Owen!' said Miss Skinner, beaming.

'Are we on the same errand, I wonder? Checking the duty files on antiquities exports?'

It had never occurred to him.

'As a matter of fact—' Then he recovered quickly. 'But I see you've got ahead of me this morning!'

'It's the obvious thing to do, isn't it? You can see at a glance what antiquities have been exported and how much duty has been paid. And do you know what I've found?'

She looked pleased.

'There has been a two hundred and sixty per cent increase in the volume in the last twelve months. There! I expect you have already spotted it but it came as a surprise to me. I suspected there had been an increase but not on this scale!'

'That is, actually, the very thing I wanted to talk to you about.'

Miss Skinner looked at her watch.

'I think I have time for a cup of coffee,' she said. 'It will give the people here a chance to find some more files for me. They seem to need,' she added, 'plenty of time.'

He took her round the corner to a little Arab café.

'I wonder if I can enlist your aid, Miss Skinner? The Government is, as you know, determined to tackle the question of the flight abroad of Egypt's national treasures—'

'The Spoils of Egypt,' said Miss Skinner, nodding her head approvingly.

'In doing so, however, it does not wish to jeopardize its excellent relations with other countries. Particularly America—'

'Since that's where the money comes from.'

'Quite. Unfortunately, something has cropped up which may send the wrong signals to your compatriots, Miss Skinner, and I wondered if by any chance we could count on your assistance in persuading the American public of our good intentions.'

'My uncle, perhaps—'

'Especially as it concerns something you know about.'

He told her where things stood on the Parker prosecution.

'The Government might, you see, wish to take up the issue of negligence, but would not wish to do so if it suggested to the community abroad that it was conducting an anti-foreign campaign.'

'I see your point.'

She was obviously considering the matter. Then she seemed to make up her mind.

'I will do what I can. All the more so as I feel a particular concern for those two poor men. A personal responsibility, you might say. Yes, you can count on me.'

Owen started to express his thanks, but she interrupted him.

'And in return,' she said, putting her hand on his arm, 'you can do something for me.'

'Of course.'

'Tomorrow afternoon I am visiting a friend. A private commission. When I get back I shall ring you and you can forget about it. If I do not ring you by four, will you please go to my hotel and there on my escritoire you will find a sealed envelope which will tell you where I have been. There! That's it.'

'But, Miss Skinner,' said Owen, bewildered, 'what then do you want me to do?'

'I am sure, Captain Owen, that, should the occasion arise, you will know very well what to do.'

CHAPTER 10

'The Expedition to Punt?' said Monsieur Peripoulin wrathfully. 'Over my dead body!'

'Over your dead body it's going to have to be, then,' said Parker. 'I've got a deal.'

'Deal? I know nothing about deals.'

'It's time you learned, then. We had this before we started. We wouldn't have started otherwise.'

'What is this "deal"?' Peripoulin asked Owen. 'I don't understand. I know nothing about deals.'

They were at the Museum. Around them on the floor were the spoils from Der el Bahari. Most had already been valued and packed away again in large wooden crates. Only the façade, complete now,—Owen had checked that the leopard cub was there—remained to be packed.

And valued.

'Not something I can do,' the under-keeper had said, and had fetched Monsieur Peripoulin.

'What is this deal?' Owen said to Parker.

'When we applied for the licence to excavate,' said Parker, 'we were given to understand that we could retain whatever we found.'

'No.' Owen shook his head. 'That couldn't have been the case. There's always a reservation. The Museum has the right to retain items of outstanding historical significance.'

'Sure, I understand that. If you find another Cow of Hathor or something, that goes to the Museum.'

'The Expedition to the Land of Punt,' said Monsieur Peripoulin. 'That is of outstanding historical significance.'

Parker shrugged.

'Yeah, well, it's all interesting.'

'This is exceptional.'

'Up to a point. The fact is,' said Parker, 'you've got to let us have something. Otherwise it wouldn't be worth doing.'

'But not the Land of Punt,' said Monsieur Peripoulin firmly.

'I tell you, we've got a deal.'

'It says you can export the Land of Punt?'

'Not in so many words,' Parker admitted, 'but—'

'This deal,' pursued Monsieur Peripoulin, 'it is in writing?'

'I dare say it's written down somewhere,' said Parker off-handedly.

'*O-oh là-là!* I know about deals like that.'

'This one's kosher,' said Parker. 'It's with the Ministry.'

'The Département? Well, that is strange. For I am in the Département and I have not heard of any such "deal".'

'You wouldn't,' said Parker. 'It was confidential.'

'Ah? It was confidential? So confidential that even I, Peripoulin, have not heard of it! That is strange indeed. Well,' said Monsieur Peripoulin, 'until I do hear of it, I shall assume it does not exist. The façade remains here!'

He stalked off.

It took Parker a moment or two to recover. Then he exploded.

'You can't do that! You can't do that! I've got a deal!'

For a moment it seemed he was about to charge after him.

'That's the most valuable piece of the lot!' he shouted.

'Precisely,' said Monsieur Peripoulin, and disappeared into his office.

Owen put a restraining hand on Parker's arm. Parker shook it off.

'What does he think he's doing? I've got a deal!'

'Have you?' said Owen.

It took a moment for the words to sink in. Then Parker quietened down.

'Yes,' he said. 'I sure have. You don't think we'd move without one, do you? There's somebody else who's interested—' He broke off. 'Well,' he said, 'there's bound to be others. But we got first strike. That was the deal.'

'That doesn't sound a Department of Antiquities sort of deal.'

'Well, it was.'

'Are you sure it was with the Department? Who did you talk to?'

Parker hesitated.

'It wasn't quite like that.' He hesitated again. 'As a matter of fact, we didn't approach them directly ourselves. We did it through people with influence—'

'Oh yes,' said Owen sceptically.

'No, really,' Parker insisted. 'We wanted to make sure, you see. We knew there was somebody else after it, another consortium. We wanted to be sure we got it. So we went to the top.'

'Peripoulin's the top.'

'No, no. Higher.'

'Who?'

Parker was silent.

'You've been sold a pup,' said Owen.

Parker shook his head.

'No, I haven't. Don't think I haven't done this sort of thing before. I know what to look out for.'

'Well,' said Owen, 'Peripoulin's not going to change his mind.'

Parker looked at him.

'Can't he be made to?'

'Not by me, if that's what you're asking. It would have to be by the people you made the deal with, the people at the top. If they really are at the top.'

'Well, they are,' said Parker.

'Why don't you call on the services of your friend again? The man with influence?'

A little to his surprise, Parker took him seriously.

'Yes,' he said. 'Why not?'

He went off to find a phone. Owen thought for a moment of eavesdropping, but it was too late. Then something else occurred to him.

He made his way along the corridor to the main office of the Museum. He wanted to make a phone call himself.

Abu Bakir answered it.

'The Department of Antiquities?' he said. 'But I'm in Finance. Why ask me?'

'I thought you might have friends there.'

There was a little silence.

'I'll see what I can do,' he said.

Owen went back to the room with the crates. He found two people looking at the façade: Francesca, the Italian girl from Alexandria, and Tomas, the Copt.

'Hello,' he said. 'I didn't realize you two knew each other.'

'Hello,' said Francesca. 'I know you, too. But I've known Tomas for even longer.'

Tomas smiled politely.

'I'm glad you've been able to locate the leopard cub,' Owen said to him.

'Leopard cub?' said Francesca, puzzled.

Owen pointed the fragment out to her.

'It got parted from the others.'

Francesca raised an eyebrow.

'At Heraq. You remember.'

'I see,' said Francesca, and laughed.

'It was a mistake,' said Tomas.

'It certainly was,' said Francesca. 'It would have reduced the value of the façade considerably.'

'What *is* the value of the façade?' asked Owen.

'Impossible to say on a thing like that. I expect the Museum's put a value on it, though.'

'I think there's some difficulty about that.'

'Oh. I see! Alphonse.'

'Alphonse?'

'Peripoulin.'

'That's right.'

'He doesn't want to let it go?'

'Can you blame him?'

The girl shrugged.

'I've seen so many nice things leave Egypt,' she said.

'The Land of Punt, I would have thought, was special. Unique. Priceless.'

'Not priceless,' the girl corrected him. 'And not even a particularly high price as these things go. It would only be of interest to museums. What really fetches the money are smaller things—things that would fit into a private collection.'

'Like the Cow of Hathor?'

'That, thank goodness, is safe here. But yes, like the Cow of Hathor.'

'I like the Land of Punt. I hope Peripoulin wins.'

Tomas, who had been standing quietly by, stirred a little.

'Yes,' said the girl, 'we ought to get on with it. Only we can't really, not until the business about the façade is settled.'

'You could take the others,' Tomas suggested.

'I suppose I could. And come back for the façade. I'll be here again next week.'

'Why are you taking them?' asked Owen.

'What do you mean?'

'Why you and not Tomas?'

'Tomas is just a contractor. Well, not just. It's a skilled business transporting these. But his work finishes when he gets it to the Museum. After that, I take over.'

'It's different,' said Tomas. 'The first part is hauling and carrying. The second part is forms.'

'That's me,' said the girl. 'Coming from Italy, I know all about forms. And bureaucracy.'

Tomas gave her a sheaf of papers.

'It's all here,' he said, glancing round at the crates and then, surreptitiously, at Owen. 'Now.'

'Right, then. I'll get the porters to move it.'

She walked briskly out. Tomas shook hands politely with Owen.

'What are you doing now? Going back to Der el Bahari?'

'For the next load,' said Tomas.

Francesca reappeared with a string of porters.

'These, and these,' she said. 'And I've got some more stuff next door. From other customers.'

'All to the depot?'

'To the depot. We have a small warehouse,' she explained to Owen. 'We sort the things out there, in Alexandria, before taking them along to Customs.'

'This one?' asked the leader of the porters, pointing to a large package touched up with gilt paint, which almost blocked the doorway.

'My goodness, yes. Be careful! It's a nice one. And don't get it mixed up with these.'

The man bore it off. It wasn't long before all the crates had been cleared away. Only the façade was left, lying pieced together jigsaw-like on the floor.

'I'll leave you to guard it,' said Francesca, coming to shake hands.

'You're returning to Alexandria?'

'Tomorrow afternoon. Tonight I am giving myself a treat. *Cavalleria*. I don't suppose . . . ?'

'I am already engaged to go there. But perhaps at the interval?'

The telephone in Peripoulin's office gave a long ring. After a moment Peripoulin emerged slowly. Parker came into the room.

'Satisfied?' he said to Peripoulin triumphantly.

'No,' said Peripoulin. 'Not satisfied.'

He came over to the façade and stood looking down at it.

'Well?'

Peripoulin ignored him and addressed himself to Owen.

'I have been asked to put a value on this,' he said. 'I do so: one million pounds.'

*

Zeinab was unaccountably out of sorts at the opera that evening: and that was before they met Francesca.

The Opera House had been built by the Khedive Ismail as part of his lavish preparations for the Grand Opening of the Suez Canal. Inside, all was crimson and cream and gold. The boxes, most of which were harem-style, screened to preserve the harem ladies from the gaze of the licentious, were fitted out with red brocade. And one of them was the special perquisite of the Mamur Zapt.

When, on taking up his post, Owen had first discovered that he possessed this private privilege, he had been surprised and touched. What an imaginative, what a civilized way of rewarding service, he had thought!

Of course, it was nothing of the kind. The Khedive Ismail had been determined to make his venture a success and one way of doing it was to guarantee the attendance of the elite. All his Ministers had boxes and woe betide them if they did not attend. The Mamur Zapt, the Chief of the Khedive's Secret Police, was there in person to make sure that they did.

Cultural standards had declined so much, of course, with the coming of the British that this was no longer one of Owen's duties. And the Mamur Zapt's box might have gone forever unused had he not discovered, when he met Zeinab, that this was about the one part of the Mamur Zapt's office that she took seriously.

Since then they had been assiduous attenders and Owen had come to the conclusion that the Welsh, the Arabs and the Italians had significant things in common, most notably a taste for emotional drama which other, colder nations—the English, for example—would call facile.

Normally, Zeinab succumbed to the spell the moment she entered the House. This evening, though, she seemed to surrender herself to the music slowly and almost unwillingly.

'Feeling all right?' asked Owen solicitously.

If she was, this soon altered when they went downstairs at the interval and Owen greeted effusively this tall, beautiful, elegant, European girl.

'We met at Alexandria,' Owen explained.

'Oh!' said Zeinab.

'So nice to see you yesterday,' said Francesca.

'Yesterday?' said Zeinab, with raised eyebrows.

'At the Museum.'

'In Cairo too, then.'

'My work takes me there,' Francesca explained.

'Work?' said Zeinab.

This was strange and suspicious. Women did not work. Not unless they were peasants. And this girl was plainly not a peasant.

'I run an antiquities business.'

'That's how we came to meet,' Owen explained.

'Oh? Since when have you been interested in antiquities?'

'Since I got landed with this business about export licensing.'

This time it was Francesca's eyebrows which were raised.

'You didn't tell me about this,' she said.

'There are lots of things he doesn't tell people about,' said Zeinab.

Both women grew cool, and not just towards each other. In an effort to improve matters, Owen talked to Francesca about the opera they had both seen at Alexandria. Zeinab became even cooler.

Owen felt obliged to explain how they had come to meet at the Opera.

'By the way,' said Francesca, 'have you reached a decision yet on the statue?'

'Not yet.'

'The person we would use has a studio here in Cairo. Would it help you to see the sort of work he does?'

'That's not really the point, actually—' Owen began, but Zeinab cut in.

'I am against statues,' she said.

'But they can be so beautiful!' Francesca cried.

'Not in Egypt they can't,' said Zeinab.

Francesca shrugged.

'But surely Egypt is looking outwards now? Opera itself—'

'Egypt is for the Egyptians,' said Zeinab and moved towards the stairs.

Francesca put her hand on Owen's arm.

'Do come and see!' she said. 'Vittorio would be so pleased. He's in the Sharia el Nazdafni. I'll meet you there at ten o'clock outside the mosque.'

Zeinab was silent for the rest of the evening; silent but stormy.

'Dante!' said Vittorio next morning. 'Ah, Dante! It would not be work, it would be homage.'

His studio was on the roof of an old, crumbling house and opened, as did many of the houses, on to a small roof garden. There were blocks of limestone everywhere. Beyond a trellis covered with heavy swathes of bean flowers, the tips of an angel's wings rose incongruously.

'Much of my work is funerary,' said Vittorio sadly, following Owen's eye. 'I don't get many commissions. Were it not for Francesca—'

'It is a shame,' said Francesca, 'because his work is really very good. Let me show you.'

She took Owen back into the studio and showed him several half-finished fragments rather like the ape-god he had seen in the Customs House at Alexandria.

'Truly lovely,' she said, running her hand admiringly over the head and shoulders of a cat which was emerging from the still untrimmed block below.

'And what about this?'

It was a remarkable sculpture of the Vulture Goddess Mut, with spread, delicately-feathered wings and crooked, powerful talons holding in them the plumes of Upper and Lower Egypt. The detail was amazing.

'I flatter myself,' said Vittorio proudly, 'that you couldn't tell the difference.'

'The Dante, though, would be an original,' said Francesca.

'Yes,' Vittorio asserted. 'I have thought about it a little. Just on the off-chance, you know. Let me show you some of my sketches.'

'Very fine,' said Owen after a while, handing them back to him. 'I am, of course, no expert but even I can see—'

'Put this up,' said Francesca passionately, 'and in years to come people will say this is one of the treasures of Alexandria!'

'The treasures of Egypt, I see,' said Owen to Vittorio, 'are not all in the past!'

Vittorio bowed.

'I do not understand,' he said sadly, 'why people should object. An artist makes with respect. How can what is made with respect be seen as insult or blasphemy?'

'Different people see things in different ways,' said Owen neutrally.

And how was he going to explain this visit to Zeinab?

As Owen was walking back to his office he met one of his old friends, last seen proffering ushapti images outside the Continental Hotel.

'You still here?' said Owen, surprised.

The last tourists had departed. The summer heat had finally closed down on the city and the Season was over. There were fewer porters now outside the great hotels. Many of them had returned to their homes in Upper Egypt for their annual visit, bringing gifts for their wives and children. The great bazaars were almost empty.

'I shall go home next week,' said his friend.

'Sold all your stock?'

The man grimaced.

'Some of it. I should have come up here earlier, before the others. I stayed on the boats too long.'

They said that every year. The fact was, when they moved, they all moved together, like a flock of starlings. They all came together and left together.

That was strange. The flock had, in fact, already departed, returning to the south to replenish their energies and their stock for next season.

'You're a bit late, aren't you?'

'I had some things to do.'

'A wedding, perhaps?'

Some of the pedlars were like sailors: they liked a wife in every port.

The man laughed.

'No,' he said, 'not this time. There are some things I have to do for the Pasha.'

'Oh!' said Owen. 'You are rising in the world, then?'

'I wouldn't say that.'

'Does not the Pasha have his own men?'

'For most things. For some things, though, he likes to make use of the people from Der el Bahari.'

'And what sort of things are they?'

'Ah. Specialist things.'

Owen would have liked to have known what they were but he knew better than to ask.

'I was at Der el Bahari last week,' he said. 'Had I known that I would run into you I would have asked after your family.'

The man bowed acknowledgement.

'It is a long time to be separated from them.'

'Were you not tempted to work at the dig, too?'

'No. That work is too close to working in the fields to suit me.'

'Profitable, though.'

The man shrugged. 'You have to work hard. Besides, I don't like working for the American.'

'The accidents?'

'Accidents? Oh no. They were to people from outside the village.'

'Isn't it the work? Dangerous?'

'No!' the man scoffed. 'It wasn't that at all!'

'What was it, then?'

'They were asking for it, weren't they?'

'Were they?'

Owen probed but the man suddenly shut up like a clam. After a little while they both laughed.

'You Der el Bahari people stick together, don't you?' said Owen.

'We have to.'

Owen took this to be a reference to the illicit traffic the villagers engaged in.

'Well,' he said, 'from what I saw, there's plenty more stock left for you.'

He told the man about the mummies.

'Oh yes,' the man said. 'There are hundreds of those. It's the smaller objects you can't lay your hands on these days. In my grandfather's time you could still do all right. Lamps, jars, ushabti, even the occasional necklace. But that's all disappeared long ago.'

'And if there's something big, I suppose it's the archæologists who find it.'

'Oh, I wouldn't say that. We know our way around. Those archæologists are digging blind. Doesn't make much sense, in my view. They're not going about it properly.'

'The wrong methodology?' murmured Owen.

'What's that? All I know is, I wouldn't set about it the way they do. No, that's not the problem. The problem from our point of view is not finding, but selling. If you let anyone know you've got your hands on something big, the next moment the Government comes and takes it away from you. Or maybe it's the Pasha, if you don't look out. Any way there's nothing in it for us.'

'It's a hard life,' said Owen.

'It certainly is. And unfair, too. We've been doing all right for centuries and then along comes some new Government or other and mucks it up. It's unjust, that's what it is. The Government's either on your back or in your pocket.'

'I can see you've got problems.'

'The lengths you have to go to!' said the man from Der el Bahari.

'No,' said Zeinab.

This was serious. Normally, Owen, mad dog that he was, dispensed with a siesta and worked right through. Today, though, it was so hot that it was impossible. Even indoors it was like an oven. The fans blew air at you that was like heat from an exhaust. So at lunch-time he had gone to Zeinab's. Zeinab, however, was not in the mood.

'You come to me as if I were a harem,' she said. 'A harem of one, perhaps—you English are peculiar—but still a harem. Why don't you go to that Francesca of yours?'

'She's not mine. You're mine.'

'I'm not so sure about that,' said Zeinab. 'And if I am, it's probably not going to be for much longer.'

'What's that?'

'It's spelt E-N-D,' said Zeinab.

'What nonsense!' said Owen, trying to put his arm round her. She shrugged it off. 'You're not seeing things in proportion.'

'What was the proportion you had in mind?' asked Zeinab. 'Fifty-fifty? Or seventy to Francesca and thirty to me?'

'For God's sake!'

This time he did succeed in getting his arm round her.

'It's no good,' said Zeinab, suddenly tearful. 'My father has been.'

Owen sat back.

'What's he got to do with it?'

'He thinks it's time I got married.'

'Married!'

Owen sat back still further. 'He's never bothered about that sort of thing before!'

'It's not that. He thinks that, well, there may be a use for me.'

Light dawned.

'Marbrouk?'

Zeinab nodded.

'Suddenly they are great friends. And he wishes to cement the alliance.'

'With you as the cement? Not likely!'

'It is quite normal between great families. And Marbrouk belongs to a great family. He is a cousin of the Khedive. If he murdered about sixty of his relatives, which of course he is quite capable of doing, I might find myself wife to the Khedive.'

'Bloody hell!'

'*One* of the wives of the Khedive,' said Zeinab, gratified. 'Which is, admittedly, a drawback.'

Owen could see it all. That wily, conniving Nuri was quite capable of using his daughter as a pawn in some political game he was playing. Marbrouk and Nuri! Christ, they might be planning to take over the Government!

'We're not having this!' he said.

'I don't know what it's got to do with you,' said Zeinab, a trifle smugly.

'It's got plenty to do with me,' said Owen. 'I'm in love with you, aren't I?'

'Francesca.'

'She's not in it.'

'Oh dear,' said Zeinab. 'I thought she might be a consolation when I'm gone.'

'You're not going,' said Owen.

Zeinab, enjoying this, curled her legs up under her on the divan.

'It would be a good match,' she said dreamily. 'He is a millionaire. And you still have some way to go. Nine hundred and ninety-nine thousand pounds, to be exact. He is, of course, older than you. But then, his place in society is already established and his wife could expect to take her position beside him—'

'Not in Egypt she couldn't.'

'True. But then my position at the moment is not exactly one to be proud of, is it?'

'There's more to life than position,' said Owen stiffly.

'Yes,' said Zeinab, suddenly serious. 'I have been reflecting on that. Has it ever occurred to you that I might wish for more from life than to be mistress of a junior Captain in the British Army? To marry, for instance, and have children?'

'I thought you were happy.'

'I have been happy,' said Zeinab. 'Now I am wondering.'

Expelled from Zeinab's bosom, Owen went back to his office. He felt he needed to think things over and there, at any rate, he would be able to do it in peace. The great building was completely empty. The bearers were asleep in the yard, the clerks asleep at home. Even Nikos, his official Clerk and Office Manager, had taken himself off.

A single telephone was ringing determinedly. He picked it up. It was Abu Bakir.

'Captain Owen: could we meet? I would like to introduce you to two of my friends.'

'This evening some time?'

'Now would be better. We are in a café. If you come to the Bab-es-Zuweyla I will meet you.'

When Owen arrived at the Old Gate with its tall minarets and its weapons of the Afrit giant high on its sides, he
found Abu Bakir waiting. They went down a little alleyway
behind the Gate and ducked into a tiny one-room café in
which two men were sitting at a low table.

'This is Hafiz,' said Abu Bakir. 'I will not say where he
works but he will answer your question about who contacted the Department of Antiquities this morning.'

'Thank you, Hafiz,' said Owen. 'But can you tell me first
who it was who rang Parker at the Museum?'

'Abd el Ta'arquat,' said the man immediately.

'Who is he?'

'The under-secretary.'

'And, presumably, someone rang him?'

'Yes.'

'Who was it?'

Hafiz gave Abu Bakir a quick glance. Abu Bakir nodded.

'A Pasha.'

'Marbrouk?'

Hafiz looked surprised.

'No,' he said, 'not Marbrouk.'

'Who, then?'

'Sidki Narwas Pasha.' He hesitated. 'And another rang
after.'

'Who?'

'Raquat Pasha.'

Where had he heard the names before?

'Pashas,' he said.

'I told you,' said Abu Bakir. He turned to the other man.
'This is Naguib,' he said.

The other man bowed and shook hands. He was dressed,
despite the heat, in a dark suit and wore, like Hafiz, the
tasselled tarboosh of the effendi. Both were, presumably,
civil servants and both, he suspected, in view of their connection with Abu Bakir, Nationalists.

'You asked another question,' said Abu Bakir.

'I did?'

'Earlier. You asked me who it was who had complained to the Ministry of Justice about Mr el Zaki's investigation. Naguib will tell you.'

'Their names only,' Naguib stipulated.

Owen nodded.

'Very well.'

'Sidki Narwas Pasha.'

'And Raquat Pasha?'

Naguib shook his head.

'Marbrouk,' he said.

Owen went back to his office and stayed there for the rest of the afternoon. By four o'clock he had still not heard from Miss Skinner, so he went round to her hotel and there, on her escritoire, he found the sealed envelope. He pulled out the letter inside.

Dear friend [it said],

In case of accidents (they have been so frequent, haven't they?) I would like you to know that I have gone (does this surprise you? Really?) to Heraq.

CHAPTER 11

Owen took a police launch this time. It was less picturesque than a felucca, but more speedy. He also took with him three constables, two police trackers and a fat Greek. The Greek was used to this sort of thing and his name was Georgiades.

He was not, however, used to going out of Cairo and as the levees dropped away and revealed the plots and the plantations, the small boys on their oxen driving the water-wheels, the men up to their shins in mud coaxing the water through the fields, and the women statuesque with pots on their heads, he looked around with interest, especially at the women.

He was, however, listening and when Owen came to a stop he said with definiteness:

'We'll start at the house.'

When they arrived at Marbrouk's house, though, they found it shut up and shuttered. This presented no problem to Georgiades, nor, indeed, to Owen, who as Mamur Zapt had right of entry without warrant to all premises in Cairo and reckoned that this counted as Cairo, with a bit of stretching.

Georgiades prised open a door and they went in. All was cool and dark and sumptuous. The floors were tiled and rich carpets hung on the walls. Apart from that there was little furniture, merely a few low tables and low divans. In every room though, there were alcoves in which was an amazing collection of works of art. Unusually for an Arab —most rich modern Arabs despised the non-Arab past— most of them were Pharaonic. It was like walking through the Museum.

Georgiades was not interested in works of art but in cellars and locked rooms. He was casually forcing open one of the latter when some men rushed in.

'What are you doing?' they shouted.

'I'm looking for a woman,' said Georgiades. 'Perhaps you can tell me where I can find her?'

The men froze.

'Take them out,' Georgiades said to the constables. 'Put them in the yard.'

When Owen went out a little later there was quite an assembly in the yard.

'This is the Pasha Marbrouk's,' someone called out. 'You will pay for this.'

'This is the Mamur Zapt,' said one of the constables,

'and I am Ibrahim, and the next time you speak out of turn, you will pay for it, too.'

The trackers came into the yard looking at the ground.

'Did you find anything?' Owen asked.

'Oh yes,' they said. 'She's been here twice, once a few days ago—but you know that, don't you, because we saw that you were here, too—and then again today. She went into the house.'

'Was there anyone with her?

'No.'

They fanned round the house. After a moment one of them called Owen over.

'The house was shut,' he said. 'Look, this is where she broke in.'

'It was shut when she came?'

'The servants were at the back, I expect.'

The trackers looked into the house but did not come inside. Outside, their skills were incredible. They could track a man and a camel for five hundred miles across the desert and then pinpoint him in a crowded market. Inside, where there was no sand, they were lost.

'What about Marbrouk? Can you see his steps?'

'He left the day, you left.'

'And has not been back?'

'No.'

They shook their heads definitely.

Owen rejoined Georgiades. They were talking in one of the rooms when there was a tap on the shutter.

'Effendi!' It was one of the trackers.

Owen opened the shutters.

'Some men came. They seized her, we think, and took her away.'

Owen went out. The trackers were standing by a small rear door, a servant's entrance, heavily padlocked. They indicated the ground at their feet. All Owen could see was scuffed sand.

'You can see they were carrying something when they came out. It was not heavy but it was . . .' The tracker hesitated.

'Like a goat,' said the other tracker.

'Yes. Wriggling.'

For that, at any rate, Owen was thankful. He took the trackers back into the yard.

'Are any of these men,' he said, 'the men who took her?'

The trackers walked round looking at the men's feet.

'No,' they said.

'They were different sort of men,' one of the trackers offered.

'From the city?'

'Oh no.'

'Bandits?'

'No.'

'What sort of men, then?'

The trackers conferred.

'They came from the country,' they said, 'but are not from the country. Not now.'

'They no longer work on the land?'

'That is right.'

The trackers went back to the scuffle marks and then began to walk off, heads bent, into the orange trees.

Georgiades went over to the servants who had rushed in.

'Those men my friends were talking about,' he said: 'they went in through the little door.'

The servants looked at him dumbly.

'It was locked. But you, I think, have the key.'

'We don't know anything about it.'

'You use the door. You have the key.'

'There can be more than one key,' one of the servants objected.

'My friends, when they get back, will be able to tell where they went to fetch the key. You could save them, and me, and the Mamur Zapt, a lot of time by telling us now where I can find those men—and the woman. You can also,' he added, as the men showed no signs of responding, 'save yourselves even more time: the time which you will spend in the caracol if you do not help the Mamur Zapt.'

The servants looked distinctly uncomfortable but did not reply. They were the Pasha's men and if they did something against his interests could expect a fate much worse than the caracol.

Owen was just turning back to follow the trackers when he heard an unexpected noise. It came closer and closer and then into the yard swept a bright, shining motor-car. It was driven by a chauffeur and in the back was Zeinab's father, Nuri Pasha.

'*Mon cher!*' cried Nuri, disconcerted but recovering. 'What a surprise! What an agreeable surprise!'

'It is indeed, *cher Pasha!* But tell me, dear friend, what is it that brings you here so far from Cairo on such a hot evening?'

'Love,' said Nuri firmly.

'Love?'

'Are you surprised? My friend, I would have thought it was obvious.'

'For Miss Skinner?'

'Who else?'

Owen could think of quite a few others. However . . . 'For Miss Skinner, of course. But then in that case, Pasha, perhaps you can tell me how you know she was here?'

'She told me,' said Nuri, wide-eyed.

'Told you? When?'

'When she borrowed my car,' said Nuri, linking his arm, father-like, through Owen's.

'Well, of course, I wasn't too happy about it, my dear fellow. After all! I knew Marbrouk's feelings, well, let's not say feelings—Marbrouk is a rough and ready fellow, it's in the family, a bit too much of the Mameluke, I would say

—let's say *urges* with respect to Miss Skinner. Ought I to allow her to go alone? I did point this out to Enid—'

'Enid?'

'Miss Skinner. However, she felt my presence might be misconstrued and was positive that she could handle all eventualities, so in the end I was reluctantly persuaded. But then when the car came back—'

'The car came back?'

'Yes. Ali—that's my chauffeur—was told it would not be needed. Well, my dear fellow—what was I to think? No business of mine, you will say, and of course you are right. On the other hand! A delicate lady, unused, perhaps, to our boisterous ways—well! And then I questioned my chauffeur and learned that it was not actually Miss Skinner herself who had dismissed him but some crude, rough fellows. Well, I was a teeny bit worried, I don't mind admitting, and so—well here I am!'

'Reassuring for her, no doubt. If, that is, she were here.'

'Not here?' Nuri stopped. He waved a hand towards the house.

'Closed. Shuttered.'

Nuri's face hardened. 'In that case, my dear fellow . . .'

He produced a small pistol from his pocket.

'Ali!'

The chauffeur climbed out of the car. He was wearing pistols on both hips and had a dagger stuck in his belt. He reached back under the dashboard and produced a shotgun.

'You stay where you are,' said Owen, and ran off in the direction the trackers had taken.

Through the orange trees he could see a little stone building. Georgiades was standing beside it. As Owen ran up, he picked up a huge stone and crashed it against the door.

'Again!' commanded a voice from inside.

'Miss Skinner,' said Owen: 'are you all right?'

There was a silence inside.

'Why, it's the ever-reliable Captain Owen! Perfectly, thank you. Well, perhaps not perfectly—'

'Stand aside, my dear,' said Nuri. 'I am going to shoot out the lock.'

'No you don't!' said Owen. 'The bullets might go anywhere. You!' he said to one of the constables. 'Go back to the servants and get the key.'

'Ali!' said Nuri. 'You go with him. In case they are slow. You don't understand our ways, my dear fellow,' he said apologetically to Owen. 'They are likely to be loyal to Marbrouk and may need some encouragement. Are you all right, my dear?' he said to the door.

Miss Skinner chuckled.

'Not only all right,' she said, 'but considerably flattered.'

'Where are the trackers?' Owen asked Georgiades.

'There was a man here. He ran off. They'll get him for you.'

It took the constable, even with Ali's support, some time. The trackers returned first. They were holding between them a man in the short, knee-length white shirt and turban of the tribesman. He seemed vaguely familiar.

'Who has the key?' asked Owen.

'Abdul Mohammed,' the man said sullenly.

'Who is he?'

Through the orange trees came a little crowd. In front of them were Ali and the constable, pushing a tall man in a white galabeyah.

'That is Abdul Mohammed,' said the man between the trackers.

The procession came to a halt. Ali pushed Abdul Mohammed forward.

'You have the key?'

The man produced it reluctantly. Owen fitted it into the lock and opened the door.

Miss Skinner emerged, dishevelled and dusty but unharmed.

'*Chérie!*' said Nuri optimistically.

'Thank you,' said Miss Skinner.

'Are you all right?' asked Owen. 'Not hurt—or anything?'

'Not hurt,' said Miss Skinner; 'nor anything.'

'We'll go back to the house.' Owen indicated the man between the trackers. 'Talk to him,' he said to Georgiades. 'Keep the rest of them here,' he said to the constables.

'Do you want us to find the others?' asked the trackers.

Owen hesitated. 'Do you know how many there are?'

'Four.'

'Are they armed?' Owen asked the man the trackers were holding.

'Yes, effendi.'

Owen looked at him more closely.

'I know you,' he said. 'You are from Der el Bahari.'

The man half nodded but said nothing.

'We'll go after them later,' said Owen.

It would be two against four. The trackers had guns and knew how to use them but the constables, used for city work only, were unarmed. Owen himself never carried a gun.

As they went back through the trees they heard the sound of another motor-car approaching. It pulled up in front of the house and Marbrouk got out.

'What is going on?' he said.

'You tell us,' said Owen.

He led the way into the house and sat Miss Skinner down on a divan. Despite her appearance of self-possession, she was, he thought, a little shaken.

'Enid has been attacked,' said Nuri.

'What are you doing here?' asked Marbrouk.

Nuri kept his hand in his pocket.

'She needs some water,' he said, 'as anyone other than a savage would understand.'

'I'm all right,' said Miss Skinner.

'What has been happening?' asked Marbrouk. He looked

around for his servants but they, of course, were being held elsewhere by the constables. He went away himself and returned with a glass of water.

'Would you like to—wash up, fresh up?' he asked Miss Skinner.

'Perhaps I will,' said Miss Skinner, 'thank you.'

She put down her glass and followed him out of the room.

'A Mameluke!' said Nuri. 'A veritable Mameluke!'

Marbrouk came back.

'Please will someone tell me what has happened?' he asked.

'Miss Skinner has been attacked,' said Owen. 'In your house!'

'But what was she doing in my house?' said Marbrouk, bewildered.

'Ah, what indeed!' said Nuri.

'Are you saying you did not know that she was here?'

'*Sauvage!*' said Nuri angrily.

'Of course I did not know she was here! The last time I saw her was when she left with you. Is this one of your tricks, Nuri? Because let me tell you—'

'Shut up!' said Owen, and then, recollecting himself. 'Pasha, I can check what you say with Miss Skinner,' he warned.

'Do so!' cried Marbrouk. 'Do so!'

Something clicked inside Nuri's pocket.

'No nonsense!' warned Owen.

'There is no need for any foolishness,' said Miss Skinner, returning. 'It is as Mr Marbrouk says. He was unaware that I was returning.'

'But why have you returned?' cried Marbrouk.

'Yes, why?' said Nuri.

'Without telling me! My dear Miss Skinner! I would have been here to receive you, there would have been no need—'

'For what?' asked Owen.

Marbrouk went quiet. 'I think I am owed an explanation,' he said.

Miss Skinner sighed.

'Yes,' she said. 'I'm afraid you are.'

'I was looking,' she said to Owen, 'for a calf.'

'Calf?'

'As to Cow. As to Cow of Hathor.'

'What is this?' said Nuri.

'I have reason to believe—there were rumours in the United States—that a find had been made which almost equalled that of the remarkable Cow of Hathor. It had possibly even been part of the original tableau. There had been, it was said, not just a Cow but at least one Calf.'

'Ridiculous!' said Owen. 'Professor Naville is beyond reproach.'

'Ah yes,' said Miss Skinner, 'but—or so the story goes —this was before Naville.'

'Naville was the one who found it.'

'Are archæologists ever the first to find anything in Egypt?'

'You mean—'

'The people of Der el Bahari,' said Miss Skinner, ' have a long tradition.'

'But why, then,' said Marbrouk, 'do you not look for your Calf in Der el Bahari? Why come—like a thief—to my house?'

'Because you are the Master of the village,' said Miss Skinner.

'The village is on my estate, certainly.'

'I thought the villagers might well have approached you. It would be difficult to find a market for something as unique as this. Especially for ordinary villagers.'

'I think you have been deceiving me, Miss Skinner,' said Marbrouk.

'In the interests of mankind,' said Miss Skinner.

'Am I to take it that your entry into the house was un-authorized?' asked Owen.

'Yes,' said Marbrouk.

'I am ready to face the consequences,' said Miss Skinner.

'You will,' said Marbrouk.

'Only if I am put on trial, I shall then feel obliged to reveal all I know about Mr Marbrouk's collection. And how he came to assemble it.'

'That does not worry me,' said Marbrouk.

'It will worry Captain Owen. And the Government. Both British,' said Miss Skinner, 'and Egyptian.'

'We are left with the question of violence,' said Owen, 'the violence offered to Miss Skinner's person.'

'My servants were protecting my property.'

'*Are* they your servants?'

Marbrouk paused before replying. 'I don't know,' he said. 'I know nothing about all this. Except that my house has been broken into.'

'Is it true, my dear,' asked Nuri, 'that you were looking for the Calf?'

Miss Skinner rested her hand for a moment on his.

'I am afraid, Mr Nuri, that it is. One of the things I regret is that I have made you an unknowing partner in my criminal activities.'

'Unknowing, my dear Miss Skinner,' said Nuri exuber-antly, 'but far from unwilling.'

They were sitting outside on the verandah. A halo of insects surrounded the standard lamp. A few steps beyond the verandah it was pitch dark. The grasshoppers chirruped loudly and mingled with the distant noise of the frogs by the river. Occasionally, not sufficiently far away, there was the cry of a jackal.

The servants, reluctantly released by Owen, kept the glasses well plied, although Owen himself did not drink much. He had decided that in the morning, he would have to go out after the other attackers. He would lead the party himself and supplement it with Nuri's militant chauffeur. They would go early.

'You Americans are a little unfair on us, my dear,' Nuri was saying to Miss Skinner. 'First you ruin our cotton trade and then you deny us the opportunity of compensating by exporting our antiquities.'

'They are national treasures,' said Miss Skinner, 'part of your history.'

'Cannot I do with my history as I want?' asked Nuri. 'It is mine, after all.'

'It is more than yours; it is the world's.'

'Ah!' said Nuri, sighing.

'Everything has its price,' said Miss Skinner, 'or so some people say. Many of us believe, however, that some things are priceless.'

'You don't think,' said Nuri, 'that perhaps you could keep your arguments at home?'

Miss Skinner laughed. A little later, taking advantage of a moment when Nuri and Marbrouk were deep in conversation, she said quietly to Owen:

'Would it be possible for me to question the man you took yesterday? The man who was guarding me?'

'You don't speak the language.'

'I was wondering if I could borrow Mr Nuri for the occasion.'

Owen at first refused. Later, having thought about it, he told her that he had changed his mind and that she could talk to the man in the morning.

The trackers awoke him when it was still dark. By the time they were out among the trees it was sufficiently light for the trackers to see the ground, although the sun had not yet risen. It was cold enough to make him glad he wore a jacket, and the leaves as they touched his face were heavy with dew.

The two trackers walked ahead. Behind them came Owen, Georgiades, Ali and one of the constables, all somehow armed. Behind them were the other constables.

The trackers moved swiftly, hardly bothering, it seemed, to look at the ground. Most of the time they were scanning ahead of them.

Through the trees a large wooden shed appeared. Owen halted his men while the trackers went ahead. He lost sight of them among the trees. A little later he saw them beckoning and led his men up cautiously.

A man was lying on the ground outside the shed. The tracker who had hit him kept his bare foot pressed firmly on the man's back but there was no sign of movement. The man had been keeping watch; not well enough.

Inside the shed three men were sleeping. It was easy.

The trackers slipped into the shed, kicked their guns away and then stood over them. The door creaked as they opened it and the men woke up but by then it was too late.

The constables rushed in, turned them on to their faces, took their belts and tied their feet loosely together; feet before hands so that they could not run away. Their hands would be occupied keeping their woollen drawers up.

The men, however, showed no disposition to run away. They seemed stunned.

The sun had only just come up when the constables began to lead them shuffling back to the house. In its light Owen could see their faces. He knew the men of Der el Bahari very well.

Hens there were in abundance pecking about the yard, so they had boiled eggs for breakfast. Marbrouk studied Owen's prisoners without comment and announced that after breakfast he was going to see his lawyer.

When the breakfast things had been removed, Miss Skinner went down with Nuri to interview the man who had been captured earlier. He was sitting in the dust with his

back against a wall; behind which, unknown to Miss Skinner and Nuri, stood Owen and Georgiades.

'The lady would like you to answer some questions,' said
Nuri softly in Arabic, 'and if you take my advice you'll
answer them quick.'

'I'm not saying anything,' said the man.

'Don't answer, and I'll cut your balls off.'

'If I do answer, Marbrouk will cut my balls off!' protested the man.

'Ah!' said Nuri, 'but I shall cut your balls off first.' He
turned to Miss Skinner. 'He says he will be delighted to
answer any questions you may ask, my dear.'

'Oh, that's very kind of him! Do tell him that, won't you?'

'She says that in her country men's balls are a favourite
dish.'

'They are?' said the man, shaken.

'Yes. And she personally relishes them. So watch your
step. What would you like to ask, my dear?'

'I want to ask him about Abu and Rashid.'

'Abu and Rashid?'

'Two men who were killed at Der el Bahari.'

'That is a strange thing to ask, my dear. However . . .'
He turned back to the man.

'She wants to know about two men. Their names are Abu
and Rashid. Or rather, were. They were killed at Der el
Bahari.'

'Never heard of them.'

'I am sure he will remember them.'

'She says you are a liar.'

'They were supposed to have been killed in accidents. It
was on the site Mr Parker is excavating.'

'Two of Parker Effendi's men.'

'I don't know anything about it.'

'Just recently.'

'She says she likes them with sauce on.'

'I wasn't even there!'

'Where were you, then?'

'I was down at Cairo—'

'Ah! So you know about it?'

The man was silent.

'What happened to them?' asked Miss Skinner.

'What happened to them?'

'I don't know. I wasn't there, I tell you!'

'You heard. What did you hear?'

'It wasn't an accident, was it?' said Miss Skinner.

'It wasn't an accident, was it?' The man did not reply. 'Was it?' said Nuri softly.

'No,' said the man at last.

'How did it happen?'

'They were prying,' said the man hoarsely. 'They were sticking their noses in where they shouldn't.'

'So they were killed?' said Miss Skinner. Her voice went quiet.

'I wouldn't bother too much about it, my dear,' advised Nuri. 'Who were these men, anyway?'

'I'd asked them to do something for me.'

'You should have asked me,' said Nuri reproachfully.

'No, no. These were—ordinary men. Workmen. Porters. Diggers.'

'In that case,' said Nuri briskly, 'there's not much to worry about, is there?'

'It was my fault,' said Miss Skinner.

'Nonsense, my dear!' said Nuri. 'How could it have been?'

CHAPTER 12

Owen had more important things on his mind: Zeinab. He knew she had been playing with him. That did not mean, however, that things were not serious. It was quite possible that Nuri was planning a political marriage for her. And it was, unfortunately, not quite out of the question that Zeinab would go along with it.

She was her father's daughter, after all. There were limits to her independence of mind. Owen suspected that marriage might be one of them. It was so deeply rooted in family and culture that, however emancipated you might be, when it came down to it you might revert to pattern.

One of the things Owen loved about Zeinab (yes, loved) was the largeness of spirit which had put her at odds with many of the patterns of the society in which she moved. Nevertheless, he could sense how great were the pressures on her. Perhaps now she had had enough.

In this society above all a woman could not exist on her own. What she needed, she might well feel now, was a more regular position.

And what position could he, Owen, offer her? Wife to a junior Captain in the British Army? That might be an improvement on mistress but it hardly compared with wife to a Pasha at Court and possibly a Princess.

Suppose he married her and then he was killed? Well, he was a soldier and that kind of thing happened to soldiers. Where would she be then? Or what when he retired? England? Somehow he didn't see Zeinab settling down to a quiet life in the Surrey countryside. Egypt? But then he wouldn't have a place, not as a retired Captain, and he couldn't see her in some expatriate limbo either. Whichever way he looked at it, it didn't seem very promising.

But Marbrouk! Well, he reckoned he might be able to put a stop to that. Marbrouk was certainly up to something and with any luck Owen would be able to land him in jail.

Perhaps not jail: Marbrouk was a Pasha, after all. Force him to leave the country, maybe.

The trouble was, Nuri might be in it, too. Daggers drawn he and Marbrouk might be over Miss Skinner, but hand in glove they almost certainly were on other things. Owen suspected, too, that Nuri might have more need of Marbrouk than Marbrouk of him. It was Nuri, when all was said and done, who was surrendering his daughter.

But that wasn't really it. The real question was should he ask Zeinab to marry him.

A sudden thought struck him. Suppose he did marry her and they didn't like it. The Administration, at the top, was fairly liberal in its attitudes. Paul, for instance, preferred Egyptian society to expatriate or Army society. But when it came to marriage they might think differently. They might post him back to India.

By this time he had arrived at Zeinab's door and had still not made up his mind.

'I was thinking about marriage,' he blurted out, as soon as he got through the door.

'Oh?' said Zeinab, drawing her knees up in front of her on the divan and hugging them. 'Which one? The Postlethwaite woman? Miss—what was her name—Colthorpe Hartley? Or that gipsy girl, perhaps?'

'You,' said Owen.

'Or the Italian girl? The one from Alexandria, Francesca?'

'You.'

'Is this a proposal?' asked Zeinab. 'It doesn't sound very romantic.'

'I've been thinking things over—'

'How very British of you! Marriage is an affair of the head, is it, not of the heart?'

'Of course it's of the heart. But that's straightforward—'

Zeinab interrupted him.

'But this is interesting!' she said, resting her chin on her knees and looking at him wide-eyed. 'The heart is straightforward? All my life I have been reading Stendhal and Flaubert and La Rochefoucauld and to them it is not straightforward at all!'

'You know what I mean.'

'Perhaps it is as in the opera,' offered Zeinab. 'The hero is simply swept away by his passion.'

'Yes, that's about it.'

'And you,' purred Zeinab, 'you are like this? Swept away by passion?'

'Yes. Now look, let's get back to the point—'

Zeinab, disconcertingly, burst out laughing.

'And did you find it?' asked Owen.

Miss Skinner looked at him sharply.

'Did I find what?'

'What you were looking for. When you broke into the house.'

It was the evening after they had got back from Heraq. Owen had allowed Miss Skinner a decent siesta in which to recover from her experiences and then had gone round to her hotel to hear her account of them; and, this time, a truthful explanation.

She received him outside on the terrace, largely deserted now that the tourists had gone and free, too, from the vendors and tumblers and beggars who had been jostling in front of it when he last came.

'I accept,' she said, 'that I owe Mr Marbrouk an apology.'

'I think,' said Owen, 'that the Parquet will want more than an apology.'

'The Parquet? Surely there is no need—'

'I think that remains to be seen. It depends rather upon your explanation.'

Miss Skinner was silent for some time. Then she roused herself and looked Owen in the eye.

'You are quite right,' she said. 'An explanation is required. I have been remiss, perhaps, in not taking you into my confidence. But since I had such doubts—such grave doubts—about the zeal with which the Egyptian Government was approaching the whole issue—'

'The illegal export of antiquities?'

'The export of Egypt's priceless treasures, whether legal or illegal. It seemed to us, back at home in Boston, that nothing was being done and that unless something was done, quick, Egypt's marvellous heritage would soon be dissipated forever. The Egyptians seemed helpless, the British seemed content to stand by while the world flocked in to despoil. So my Society—'

'Your Society?'

'The Society for the Preservation of the World's Treasures. It is based in Boston but we draw support from all over America: Concord, Worcester . . . and then my uncle, of course. Well, we decided that if no one else was going to tackle the problem of Egypt's despoliation, we would. We raised funds to send an emissary—'

'Yourself?'

Miss Skinner bowed.

'And I must say that when I arrived, my worst suspicions were confirmed. The slackness of the Administration, the incompetence of the investigating authorities—oh, I am sorry, Captain Owen, but then as you told me, you are not in fact a member of the police—the narrow terms of reference of Customs—well, I was shocked. And so, I am afraid, I decided to play a lone hand.'

'I see.'

'Yes. And I feel now that perhaps I was in error. I should have taken you into my confidence, at least a little.'

Miss Skinner smiled at him winningly.

'Thank you. I presume that your, er, investigations led you to Der el Bahari. Why was that?'

'We had heard rumours—some of us had been approached.'

'Back in Boston?'

'Yes. There are always agents, you know, touting things to rich men.'

'And some of these things were associated with Der el Bahari?'

'That is correct.'

'Most notably, of course, the Calf?'

'Ye-es. Just rumours, of course.'

'But apparently with sufficient substance in them to make you take them seriously?'

'It was just a lead, a possible lead,' said Miss Skinner modestly.

'Which you followed up.'

'Yes.'

'Successfully?'

'Only to the extent of uncovering more rumours.'

'You did not find the Calf itself?'

'Oh no.' Miss Skinner laughed. 'Rumour, I suspect, is the only substantial thing about that particular entity.'

'You doubt if there is such a thing?'

'I'm afraid I do.'

'Then,' said Owen, 'what were you looking for when you broke into Marbrouk's house?'

Miss Skinner went still.

'Other things,' she said after a moment. 'Although the Calf may be fictitious, it doesn't mean that everything is. I was sure that Marbrouk abstracted some things for himself. Why, you yourself—'

'What things?'

'The leopard cub. The—' Miss Skinner stopped. 'You don't believe me, do you?'

'No,' said Owen.

Miss Skinner was silent for a long time. At last she raised her eyes.

'All right,' she said. 'I *was* looking for the Calf.'

'The rumours were true?'

'I couldn't be sure. The Der el Bahari people were so secretive, hostile. I felt they were protecting something. But I couldn't get near it, no matter how I tried. I offered money

but they weren't interested. That puzzled me. I thought
that surely if they wanted to sell it—'

Miss Skinner broke off.

'But then it occurred to me. They weren't interested
because they had already sold it. The only thing that was
at issue was getting it into the hands of whoever it was who
had bought it. And *that* particular trail of thought,' said
Miss Skinner, 'led me to Mr Marbrouk.'

'Their local Pasha. The man they knew.'

'A crook,' said Miss Skinner, 'but a crook they were used
to dealing with. They had, of course, supplied him with
similar things on previous occasions.'

'And so you became interested in Marbrouk's transport
arrangements?'

'Yes. Which were Parker's transport arrangements.'

'Parker was part of it?'

'I don't know.' Something came into Miss Skinner's mind
and made her change it. 'Yes, he was part of it,' she said
determinedly, 'although how great a part he played, I do
not know.'

'Transport led you to Heraq,' said Owen.

'Yes. And to the Pasha's house, I'm afraid. For that I do
owe an apology— not just to Mr Marbrouk but to the
Egyptian Government.'

'And did you find it?' Owen asked again. 'The Calf?'

'No,' said Miss Skinner, looking at him thoughtfully.

As they were brought in, Owen scrutinized their faces. One
was the one he had already recognized: the man he had
talked to in the street on his way back from Vittorio's
studio. There were other faces, though, which seemed half
familiar. Perhaps he had seen them outside the Continental
Hotel.

'You have much to tell me,' he said to them when they
were all finally assembled in front of his desk. They shuffled
and looked down, except for the one he had spoken to

previously, who, confident in their relationship, looked him straight in the face.

Owen addressed himself to him.

'Well,' he said, 'you've put me in a pretty pickle, haven't you? What am I going to do with you now? Attacking a woman, a Sitt, moreover! Worse than that, a foreign Sitt I can't explain things to.'

'We wouldn't have hurt her,' said the man.

'Well, wouldn't you? You might have killed her by that tram.'

'We didn't push her in front of it,' the man protested. 'We pushed her against it.'

'Well, that was enough, wasn't it? She might have fallen between the wheels.'

'We had to bring it home to her. We had tried scaring her off before.'

'Oh?'

'Yes, at the hotel. We tried to frighten her. We thought: "Sitts will be frightened by bits of mummy." But she wasn't.'

'Maybe she didn't recognize it as a warning.'

'We told her to go home. We said that if she persisted in sticking her nose into things, very soon she would get it busted.'

'You actually said that to her?'

'Yes. But she is a woman of fortitude. She said: "You have something I want. I will pay you well for it, better than anyone else. Why don't we talk about it?" But we didn't want to talk about it.'

'Because you had already sold it.'

'Well, yes. We had already got a deal. We didn't want anyone messing it up at this stage. Besides, the Pasha . . .' The man fell silent.

'The Pasha?' Owen prompted.

'The Pasha said she was a foolish woman but a dangerous one, and that we should try to scare her off.'

'This was in Cairo, was it? Before she went to Der el Bahari? Before even the bus?'

'Yes, effendi.'

'How did he know she was dangerous?'

The man shook his head. 'I do not know,' he said. 'Except that when he spoke to us it was as if she was already known to him.'

Owen went across to the window and poured himself a drink from the large earthenware pitcher which stood on the sill, as in all Cairo windows, to cool. The water was as hot as if it had just come out of the hot water tap.

'But then at Der el Bahari she was attacked again,' said Owen. 'Can you tell me about this?'

'No. I was still up here at the time.' He looked at the others. 'We were all up here, I think.'

The other men nodded.

'Nevertheless, you may have heard something.'

The man shrugged.

Another man, gaining in confidence because of the relaxed, familiar nature of the exchanges—it was getting trapped in bewildering formal bureaucratic processes that ordinary fellahin feared, not so much the punishment itself —chipped in.

'It was the same down there,' he said. 'They didn't try to kill her. They thought killing a Sitt would be a dangerous thing. The Government would bear hard upon us.'

'It certainly would,' said Owen.

The men nodded their head approvingly. Back in the village, they had shown wisdom.

'They just pushed her into one of the chambers. If no one found her it would look like an accident. And if they did find her, well, at least she would know better.'

'She was still seeking the Calf?'

The man nodded. 'She offered money again. But by then we didn't need money. What was causing the problem was exchanging it for the Calf.'

'You still had the Calf, of course?'

The man shuffled his feet. 'There were arrangements,' he said evasively.

'Yes, and I think I know them, or at least some of them. Tell me, incidentally, how you found the Calf in the first place?'

'We're always going through the tombs. There are lots of underground passages. Some of them are blocked up, deliberately blocked, I mean, years ago by the Pharaoh's overseer. From time to time we unblock one. Only we don't really have the proper tools until the archæologists come.'

'Did you try and dispose of it without going through Marbrouk?'

'Yes.' The man shrugged. 'It's very difficult, though. You get the biggest prices abroad, and of course for ordinary villagers there's no way of contacting rich people in America—'

'So in the end you had to go through Marbrouk?'

'Yes. He beat us down, of course. He always does. But that's the way of things. The rich are powerful and the poor have to work for a living.'

The heat in the office was almost unbearable. It was hot anyway but now with all the men in it the temperature had risen until it was overwhelming. Owen had thought of questioning the men in the yard but he wanted them to feel just a little disoriented. He knew, however, he wouldn't be able to go on much longer. One or two of the men, used to heat though they were, seemed on the verge of fainting.

'Only a little more,' he said, 'then I will have you taken downstairs into the yard and you can have a drink. First, though, there is this: the Sitt was not the only one, was she, who came searching for the Calf?'

The little row of men shuffled uneasily. Everyone looked at the ground.

'Two men: Abu and Rashid. They came searching, too. Only they were killed.'

There was complete silence.

'We weren't there,' muttered one of the men.

'I know; and therefore you can talk to me without fear.'

The men kept their eyes fixed on the ground.

'These were ordinary men,' said Owen, 'fellahin like you. Why was it necessary to kill them?'

Still not a word.

'They had wives and children, like you. Life is hard without a man.'

The man he had met in the street was sweating profusely. He wiped his face with his sleeve.

'They were spies,' he said in a strangled voice.

'Who for?'

'We do not know. The Pasha said there were others who were looking for the Calf and we must see they did not take it from us.'

'Abu and Rashid: did they find the Calf?'

'No. But we were afraid they might.'

Another silence.

'They were traitors,' said another of the men hoarsely. 'They were the Pasha's men, like us. And they were working for someone else.'

'They seemed to know something—to know what to look for. Perhaps they had already found something out. It—it was important they should not go back and tell.'

'Who was it?' asked Owen. 'Who did it?'

The men did not reply. He had not expected them to.

'I was hoping, Pasha,' said Owen, 'that you would help me.'

'Is it not time, Monsieur le Mamur Zapt,' said Marbrouk, 'that you started helping *me*?'

'I would be glad to do so, Pasha. But first you must tell me what you know.'

'About what?'

'The Calf, for a start.'

Marbrouk shrugged. 'Rumour,' he said, 'mere rumour.'

'But with sufficient substance in it for you to approach possible buyers overseas.'

Marbrouk laughed. 'That still doesn't make it anything more than rumour,' he said.

'No? Are you saying you went to the trouble of contacting possible buyers merely on the off-chance that the Calf existed?'

'I'm not saying I contacted possible buyers.'

'There was no deal with the villagers at Der el Bahari?'

'A deal? With fellahin? Preposterous! My dear fellow, you forget you are talking to a Pasha.'

Owen was silent. At the moment it would still be only their word against his. And his was the word of a Pasha.

'Deal?' said Marbrouk, watching his face. 'Bizarre! And that goes for all that stuff about the Calf, too. The stuff of fiction! Purely imaginary. No, my dear fellow,' said Marbrouk, shaking his head, 'before we can talk about Calves, you'll have to convince me there ever were such a thing. Produce the Calf, my dear Owen, produce the Calf; then we can talk.'

It was midday by the time Owen reached Alexandria and the city was already shutting up shop for its siesta. He took a carriage, nevertheless, to the depot and arrived just as it was closing.

Francesca, talking to a workman at the door, looked round.

'Captain Owen!'

'Forgive me for catching you just at this moment, but I was anxious to see some of the packages you brought with you from Cairo. They have not gone through Customs yet?'

'No, we are taking them tomorrow. But why—?'

'The Parker packages especially.'

Francesca thought a little and then smiled.

'I see. You are afraid another piece of façade may have gone missing?'

'That sort of thing, yes.'

'The façade, of course, is still at the Museum. Alphonse refuses to release it.'

'Good for him.'

'But come in!'

She led the way back into the warehouse. It was full of crates, many of which he thought he recognized, the one with the gilt paint, certainly. And there, a large pile occupying most of the space in the warehouse, were the packages containing the spoils of Der el Bahari.

'You realize they are all boxed up, don't you?' said Francesca. 'We can't open them now that they've left the Museum? It can only be done in Customs. Though perhaps if you're the Mamur Zapt—'

'No,' said Owen, 'no, I don't think it will be necessary to do that. They go on to Customs tomorrow, you say?'

'Yes. I've got the paperwork here if you want to take a look at that. You could go through matching the boxes— to make sure they're all there, I mean.'

'Thank you.'

He gave the papers to Georgiades. The Greek began to work his way through the packages, examining each carefully.

'I don't think he'll find they've been tampered with,' said Francesca. 'We have a good name.'

'I'm sure you have. And I'm sure it's deserved.'

Georgiades moved on to the next group of packages. Francesca looked at her watch.

'This is going to take some time,' she said.

'Please don't let me keep you from your siesta.'

'I was thinking of lunch and wondering—there's a nice little place round the corner.'

'It would be a pleasure,' said Owen.

'What about me?' said Georgiades plaintively. 'Don't I get any lunch?'

'There's a Greek restaurant nearby,' said Francesca. 'Shall I get him to send you something?'

'Why don't I just go there?' asked Georgiades.

'OK,' said Owen, 'we'll pick you up on the way back. Can we make sure it's all locked up, though?'

'I'll give you the keys,' said Francesca, handing them to Georgiades. 'This big one is for the front, the little one is for the door at the side.'

The restaurant was small, dark and crowded. The patron was Italian and so, it appeared, were most of the customers. Francesca went round the tables shaking hands. At the end she brought the patron over to Owen.

'This is Luigi,' she said.

Owen shook hands.

'Captain Owen is going to approve our statue for us.'

'Just a minute—'

Francesca gave a peal of laughter.

'On one condition!' she said to Luigi. 'That is, that you get Guiscardia here to sing next season.'

'Guiscardia!' The patron pulled a face. 'It would cost—'

And then, realizing he had been fooled, he shook his head reprovingly at Francesca.

The café had all the usual noise and bounce of an Italian café and Owen, quick to respond to atmosphere, at once found himself drawn in.

'Are you sure you are not Italian?' asked Francesca. 'You look Italian.'

'It's the Welsh in me.'

Francesca regarded him thoughtfully.

'The English I know,' she said. 'The Welsh I have yet to discover.'

'You will enjoy the experience,' said Owen.

The lunch lasted, not surprisingly, longer than he had

intended and it was quite late in the afternoon when they picked up Georgiades.

Not that Georgiades, carafe in front of him, minded.

As they approached the warehouse, Francesca suddenly stopped.

'You've left the door open,' she said accusingly.

'No, I haven't,' protested Georgiades. 'I locked it up when I went.'

The side door was slightly ajar.

'It can't be Mekhmet,' said Francesca. 'He doesn't have the keys.'

The workman came up, dusting sand out of his galab-eyah. He had been asleep under a tree.

Francesca pointed to the door.

The workman shrugged and muttered something.

'What was that?' said Owen.

He had said something about a Sitt.

Owen went quickly to the door and stepped inside.

There, bent over a packing case, was Miss Skinner.

'Oh dear. Red-handed!' said Miss Skinner.

'Again,' said Owen.

'Our thoughts have clearly been running on similar lines,' said Miss Skinner. 'You can guess what I'm looking for.'

'Not entirely similar,' said Owen. He went forward and picked up the bag of tools.

'How could I find out other than by opening?'

'How were you going to take it away, though?'

'Take it away?' said Miss Skinner. 'I'm afraid I don't quite follow.'

'That was your intention, wasn't it?'

'Certainly not! I am assisting the police. Unofficially and informally, I admit. But to suggest I had any intention of stealing—!'

'You were working for the other group, weren't you? The other people interested in buying the Calf?'

'I don't know what you mean.'

'Parker told me there was a rival group.'

'Ah, well, Parker . . .'

'There's the group he was working for. That's the American/Pasha/Marbrouk group. And there's the group you were working for.'

'I work only for the Society for the Preservation of the World's Treasures,' said Miss Skinner with dignity. 'And that, let me assure you, Captain Owen, is a perfectly respectable body.'

'You tried to buy the Calf. And then, when you found you could not, because it had already been bought, you tried to steal it.'

'That is a harsh word, Captain Owen, and one which you will have to justify in a court of law.'

'There are worse words. You employed men to help you; and they were killed.'

Miss Skinner bowed her head.

'I acknowledge that,' she said. 'It is the thing I regret most.'

She raised her eyes again.

'Of course,' she said. 'I was employing them only to assist with my investigations. There was no question of any nefarious purpose. My intentions throughout have been purely public-spirited. That, at any rate—' she smiled— 'my lawyer will maintain.'

'Two break-ins?'

Miss Skinner brushed it aside with a gesture.

'A mere trifle. When set against the success of my efforts. Prevention of the theft of a remarkable national treasure. At the very moment when it was on the point of disappearing from Egypt forever. I had hoped, I will admit, somewhat selfishly, that mine alone would be the glory. Now, of course, Captain Owen I shall have to share it with you.'

'If, that is,' said Francesca pointedly, 'the Calf is here.'

*

'Open the cases?' said the Mudir of Customs. 'By all means. At once!'

He had brought his men over to the warehouse and they fell to work immediately. They prised off the lids and opened the contents to view. Owen went round the boxes. All the spoils of Der el Bahari—except, of course, the façade —were there to see.

'But there is no Calf,' said Miss Skinner, puzzled. 'I—I don't understand. I was sure—'

'All Parker's stuff is here,' said Owen.

Miss Skinner frowned. She took the list out of Georgiades's hands, checked it and checked it again.

'Ye-es,' she admitted unwillingly, 'all Parker's stuff is here.'

She looked around the warehouse, pursing her lips. Suddenly her eyes gleamed.

'But were there not other packages which came with Parker's stuff? That one, for instance?'

She pointed at the big box with its gilt paint.

'That's my stuff,' said Francesca.

'I demand that it be opened.'

The Mudir looked at Owen. Owen nodded his head.

The sides of the packing case fell apart. Inside was a huge, glossy, buff-coloured stone Calf.

'There!' said Miss Skinner triumphantly.

Francesca walked slowly forward and ran her hand over the Calf's flanks.

'The workmanship is excellent, don't you think?' she asked Owen. 'Only Vittorio could do something like this.'

'Vittorio?'

'I deal only in imitations,' said Francesca.

CHAPTER 13

The doors on the seaward side of the shed were open and the sunlight, reflected from the waves, cast subtle moving patterns on the roof. Through the doors came the cries of sea-gulls and the strong salt smell of the sea.

A line of porters was carrying packages out through the doors to a waiting wagon. As Owen watched, a man climbed up on to the wagon and took up the reins. It set off across the quay in a cloud of dust.

'From here it goes straight to the ship,' said the Mudir of Customs. 'It will be on board in an hour or two.'

They walked back into the Customs House. Through the doors on the other side of the shed porters were carrying in more packages.

'It's a busy place,' said the Mudir approvingly.

Tarbooshed effendis scurried hither and thither, Sous-Inspecteurs circled and swooped, porters came and went. Occasionally, Owen caught glimpses of Francesca bustling around with a preoccupied air.

A Sous-Inspecteur came up and looked at the crates.

'What's this?' he said. 'They've all been opened.'

'We opened them,' said the Mudir. 'Go ahead as if we hadn't.'

The Sous-Inspecteur shrugged.

'This one,' he said, pointing, 'and this one.'

Once again, and for the last time, Owen saw the Spoils of Der el Bahari.

The Sous-Inspecteur checked them off against the list.

'OK,' he said.

The lids were put back on.

'Any more?'

'This one,' said Owen, pointing to the box with the gilt paint.

'That one, too?' said Francesca, passing by. 'Oh well . . .'

Owen went across to the Calf and ran his fingers over its side.

'It's not always easy to tell,' he said. 'Often the only way you know is by the buff of the stone. There are always roughnesses in an original.'

'You see,' said Owen to Paul, as they sat in front of a growing row of glasses at the Sporting Club, 'what she did was to switch them at the last moment. The real Calf went up from Der el Bahari with all the other stuff and was dropped off at Marbrouk's place at Heraq. She collected it from there—I actually saw her when she was there—and took it to Vittorio's studio to have it copied.'

'Another one?' said Finance, looking over their shoulder.

'Well, that would be very nice. Thank you. The real Calf was then transported straight to her depot in Alexandria. The imitation one went to the Museum, was valued, certificated and all that, and then that went on to the depot, too. So all she had to do was switch them. In fact, all she did was transfer the seal. Tricky, and had to be done well, but then she had expert workmen.'

'How about a freshener for those glasses?' asked Finance.

'Thank you. I don't mind if I do.'

'So she was part of the Marbrouk/Pasha/Parker group all the time?'

'Yes. She had the tricky role at the end.'

'Here we are! And I've brought two more along, just in case,' said Finance.

'That's very kind of you.'

'It's a pleasure,' said Finance, 'a real pleasure. After all you've done for us. Getting rid of that damned woman—!'

*

'But what have I done?' asked Miss Skinner, all wide-eyed innocence. 'Broken into two premises? I apologize at once. I am, indeed, shocked at myself. But you know the concern I feel about the loss of Egypt's treasures—'

'But what have I done?' asked Parker. 'All I was doing was doing a Pasha a favour. Hey, you're trying to get me on that licence again—'

'But what have I done?' asked Marbrouk, spreading his hands wide. 'Certainly I bought the Calf. But I was going to send it on to the Museum in the ordinary way. And then it unaccountably disappeared. Someone broke into my house, that woman, Miss Skinner—'

Only Francesca said nothing. She did, however, let it be known that she was an Italian and that she claimed the right to be tried under the Capitulatory Arrangements, which meant that she had to be tried by an Italian court, in Italy, and under Italian law. Italian law, at this time, made no provision against the illegal export of antiquities . . .

To the victor, the spoils. Owen went to see Nuri.

Nuri seemed preoccupied. He was he said, leaving for Cannes that afternoon.

'The weather, dear boy. Things are getting a bit hot here.'

Miss Skinner? He might run into her at Cannes; in fact, he rather expected to.

'I gather she will be leaving Egypt shortly.'

Miss Skinner was another one who invoked privileges.

'Your uncle? The next President?'

'I am afraid not,' said Miss Skinner. 'He lost out in the Primaries. No, Capitulatory.'

Marbrouk?

'A nasty fellow, dear boy. Take my advice and have nothing to do with him.'

But Zeinab?

Nuri shook his head dubiously.

'An independent girl. Takes after her mother. She was my favourite courtesan, you know. Never would marry me. Though I asked her to. Many times.'

Zeinab curled her legs up under her.

'I'll have to think about it,' she said. 'That's the British thing to do, isn't it?'